LEAVE NO TRACE

LEAVE NO TRACE

A. B. GIBSON

Dedication

To Dave, Ellen, Joanne, Lee and Pat.

Acknowledgements

Thank you to Brianna Maguire for your editing and
help in keeping track of the plot.

To Kevin Self, a/k/a Tornado, who overnighted with us at our home in
Harpers Ferry on his way from Georgia to Maine. He added some color to
the story and gave me some excellent trail name suggestions.

Preface

The Appalachian Trail has no hours of operation. While most people hike it during the day, there are those who prefer it at night, for the challenge. It's an opportunity to experience nature's night cycle. Maybe encounter those nocturnal animals one can't observe during the day. Others hike at night to make up for time lost in the day during bad weather.

And then there are those who hike at night because they don't want to be seen.

Prologue

The approach was skillful. Slow and steady. Each foot placed expertly on the forest floor as precisely as the one before it. They didn't make a sound. Not one snap of a twig or crackle of a leaf.

Like a Geiger counter sensing ionizing radiation, the small handheld gadget zeroed in on its prey. Closer and closer. It looked like an old iPod, but it wasn't playing music. The message sent through its earbuds told the user the target was dead ahead. *Dead. Ha-ha.*

And there he was, sitting all by himself on a log, facing the other way and silhouetted by the light of the campfire, completely unprotected. What a dope. This tech big shot would never see it coming.

The beeps were pulsing rapid fire now, time for visual corroboration, and the light from the fire made it a cinch. Even from the back the target was easy to verify. Tall, check. Black jacket, check. Backpack — supposed to be absinthe green. *What the hell kind of green is absinthe green?* Anyway, it was definitely some kind of green. So, yeah, check. Both supposed to be expensive. They probably were. How could you tell?

Time to put on the gloves. This was going to be a snap. Literally. Even for a foreigner it was hard to suppress the giggle over that double-entendre. Only a few more silent steps now, and the victim would be close enough to touch. Practiced hands positioned themselves strategically, just inches away on either side of the unsuspecting head. And in one split second they clamped down and gave a savage twist. Snap! The head flopped down and the chin struck the now dead man's chest. Nothing to it.

In the firelight, a few of the victim's belongings caught the assassin's eye. With the watch easily pried from the dead man's wrist, the rest of the corpse forfeited a few other things it wouldn't need now, either. On the way back to the path the assassin threw the gloves onto the fire and about twenty or thirty feet later, almost as an afterthought, tossed the device at the fire, too. Don't want to get caught with that thing.

The killer took off up the path at a healthy jogging pace, which quickly became a run. The departure, while not as stealthy as the arrival, didn't need to be. The mission had been accomplished.

PART ONE

1

Earlier that day

The alert caught him by surprise, the pulsing vibration sequence accompanying the sound unmistakable. He had almost reached the top of a rise in the trail when his watch received the signal and sent that gentle shock to his wrist. Plan B. The hiker knew what it meant. There had been plenty of practice sessions with the guys in his lab. They tested it in different weather conditions and under many types and thicknesses of cloud cover and at varying altitudes. And while everyone on the team was proud of the work, nobody wanted to see their ingenious warning system put to use. Initiating it meant their boss was in peril.

In a few days, William François Chillon de Beaumont would pass through Harpers Ferry, West Virginia, the mid-point in his planned hike of the twenty-one-hundred-mile Appalachian Trail from Maine to Georgia. He knew he could have hiked faster, but he wanted to savor each mile. There was no telling when he would ever have the luxury of taking off five or six months all at once again.

To the casual observer his watch looked like one of those top-of-the-line Garmin Epix trail watches — the ones with the high-resolution touch screens that displayed colored relief maps and other more elaborate GPS functions. But this was no off-the-shelf watch. While the engineers in his lab near Montreux, Switzerland, left the exterior of the watch intact, they did an extensive overhaul of the guts. The Epix gave its users a top-class signal, and Garmin its stellar reputation, by linking two satellite systems. His lab added a third for the alert feature. Only one of the ways they customized it, this was the most vital.

The alert instructed him to abort his hike, and the vibration sequence informed him he had twelve hours to get off the trail and meet up at one of the established rendezvous locations. He never thought Plan B would be needed, and when the buzzing came his heart constricted. But Will had prepared for this moment. He tapped an icon on the watch's screen to send a return signal confirming he'd received the alert, and sat down onto a fallen tree trunk to follow through on the next step in the protocol. He unzipped the lower front pocket of his backpack, and his fingers went right to it. The USB jump drive he pulled out looked ordinary enough. Again, his engineers had thought of everything. If it fell into the wrong hands, or anyone got nosey and plugged it into a computer, they'd only find a couple of playlists and a few audiobooks. But, like his watch, it was far from ordinary. He pinched both ends with his fingers and twisted it apart, revealing a cavity and its real function. A pillbox.

He stared at the contents and gulped. They were going to have to figure out how to make this capsule smaller. He put it in his mouth anyway and washed it down with an extra-long swig from his canteen. Then he activated the GPS function on his watch, which the guys at the lab loaded with enhanced maps of the trail and escape routes to those rendezvous points from virtually anywhere. Until then, Will preferred to navigate with a paper map he kept in his back pocket. Something about the feeling of the paper in his hands lent authenticity to his hike. He had folded, refolded and sat on it so many times over the past two months it was falling apart.

"Sorry, old friend," he said aloud as he slipped the map in a plastic ziplock bag and then into his backpack. "I'm going to need to retire you now. Those are the orders." He pulled up the map on his touchscreen. It only took a few seconds for him to see both his location and the nearest escape route. He swiped at the maps back and forth and fiddled with some settings a while. He knew what to do.

With a moonless night coming up an attempt to find his way out now would be foolish. If he continued hiking another twenty minutes to the shelter where he'd planned to set up camp, he could leave the next morning at daybreak and still have a couple hours to spare. He stood up and as he slung his backpack over his shoulders he heard voices coming towards him from over the rise ahead.

The voices triggered a rush of paranoia, anxiety someone had seen him respond to the signal. But he quickly came to his senses. Taking a pill and looking at your watch was hardly incriminating, and he chalked it up to being a little jumpy since the alert. Besides, the voices he heard were from a couple he'd seen hiking several hours earlier. The guy and his girlfriend were engaged in conversation, so they acknowledged each other with only smiles and nods as they passed by.

All the rings in his nose made the boyfriend hard to forget, and Will felt sure he remembered them hiking in the opposite direction. The two small daypacks they carried gave them away as day hikers. Dozens of people hiked small sections of the trail down and back during a day, and it was the end of a beautiful day. They were probably on their way back to their car.

"Relax," he said to himself as he drew in a long breath.

Suddenly, a new voice startled him. "What's up, Red Rover?" This time the hiker belonging to this voice appeared from behind, out of nowhere, and passed by him just as quickly.

"Just livin' the dream!" Will shouted after him: "What about you?"

It occurred to Will that he hadn't passed any hikers on the trail all day, and he wondered why suddenly they all seem to appear at once. Unlike the couple, this guy moved at a fast clip and didn't respond. Within seconds he was up and over the next rise and completely out of sight. Hikers Will encountered were usually friendly, and this lack of congeniality struck him as odd. Perhaps the guy just hadn't heard him. Will only caught his face for a split second, but he was certain he didn't recognize him. The hiker was as tall as Will, and he wore a beard, but that was hardly distinctive. Almost every guy out there who could grow one did. But Will figured he must have met him at some point. Otherwise, how would he know his name, Red Rover?

From the beginning, Will felt apprehensive about maintaining his anonymity on the trail. It was the one thing about his organized hike he had not thought through thoroughly. He understood hikers were generally friendly, part of the trail's charm. He was sociable, too, and he assumed it would only be a question of time before somebody recognized him during a conversation. If the news spread, it could change the whole ethos of his trip. So, while he wasn't crazy about having to lie to his fellow hikers, he knew he couldn't exactly tell the truth, either, and prepared an elaborate and fictitious backstory.

But it turned out not to be a problem. What's known among hikers as trail magic took care of him from the beginning. Literally, the beginning, the second night. He had been keeping to himself near his tent, when hikers sharing the same campsite invited him to join them at their campfire. It was dark, and Will found it awkward not to accept, so he walked over and sat down with the others. After a little friendly small talk, Daddy Longlegs introduced himself and his friend, Shoe Store. A woman seated on the stump next to him called herself Star. When they asked what they should call him, Will wasn't sure what to say.

The question reminded him of the last television interview he gave with that crazy talk show host, just before he left. She'd introduced him by mangling the pronunciation of his full name: William François Chillon de Beaumont and then she pretended to be flummoxed about which name to call him. How could he forget how she continued to milk the studio audience for laughs when she asked them to decide for her. William, or Fransoys? She deliberately mispronounced it again to the apoplectic laughter of her fans. As he had done in so many other circumstances, Will gave a polite smile and explained with his rehearsed response, that he understood it could be a little complicated. His first name was William, in deference to his American mother, and his second name was François, for his Swiss father. His American friends called him William, or Will, and his European friends and his uncle called him François. He always ended his explanation with a little practiced chuckle.

"So, take your pick. I answer to any of them!"

Real names and private lives were rarely discussed on the Appalachian Trail, nor what you did before you started, or planned to do after you left. It was one of the compelling attractions of hiking the trail — living in the present and leaving all the other stuff behind, and even if only temporarily, creating a new identity with a blank slate.

On the Appalachian Trail that blank slate began with acquiring a new name. Unless you were a day hiker, you never used your real one. A serious hiker, though, needed a trail name, and those names were usually anything but serious. As the first chance to choose their own most had fun with it. There were lots of names pulled from nature and hiking, like Strider and Bobcat. But often a hiker's outstanding trait or quirk, or even an event, might inspire one hiker to bestow a name on another. That helped explain names like Ginger and Einstein. Whether an arcane symbol or an amusing double-entendre, trail names were very much an integral part of the trail culture.

"I'm embarrassed," he stammered. "I don't have a name." It was truly a conundrum, since he'd been born with a mouthful of them.

Star had been staring intently at him since he arrived, and it made Will uneasy. He wondered if she recognized him. Then it became obvious she did, because she walked over and gazed down at him to get a better look. Will instinctively stared down at the ground and covered his face. She pulled his hand away and lifted his head up by his chin, exposing his face to the firelight and the other campers.

She studied him for what seemed an eternity. Then she announced loudly, "Whaddya mean? Of course, you have a name. I know who you are!"

He couldn't believe someone already recognized him. He gulped and braced himself for the big reveal.

"You are...you're...let me think." Then, after a dramatic pause she announced, "You're Red Rover!"

The light from the campfire could not match the light of his smile. Red Rover. What a relief! Having a trail name made everything so easy. Forget all his other names. From now on, he was Red Rover.

He wasn't what anyone would call a traditional redhead, like his mother. His hair was more dark auburn with red undertones, or so his hair stylist always told him. When he modeled as a teenager in Milan, his agency even insisted he use a certain shampoo to accentuate the highlights. It could have been the undertones, or maybe the light from the campfire hitting him just so. Maybe it was his face, red with embarrassment. Whatever the reason, the name Red Rover felt perfect. He loved both the name and the anonymity.

Over the course of his thirty years, Will achieved celebrity status twice. As a teenager, his younger face was ubiquitous in magazine spreads and billboards, and later as a high-tech superstar, with guest appearances on television talk shows. When his friends teased him about his picture moving from ads deep inside magazines to their front covers, he sloughed it off, suggesting those covers were on tech magazines only nerds like him read. Still, there was that cover of <u>People</u>. So far on the trail, though, he remained a complete unknown. Nobody gave him a second look. He found it refreshing, and perhaps, a little humbling.

As his uncle liked to say, it was all about context. Who would expect a famous tech billionaire to be hiking the Appalachian Trail solo?

2

By the custom ringtone, she knew she had to answer the call immediately. And it must be important. Geneva was six hours ahead, and it would be four a.m. for the caller. Suzen Movora, just entering her apartment, found answering her phone wasn't going to be so easy. First, she needed to finish dragging her large suitcase the rest of the way through the doorway, so she could close the door behind her. Then she had to step around it in the dark. She hoped the phone would keep ringing long enough for her to extricate it from her purse, pinned under a second shoulder bag. She snickered at how comic it would have looked.

Alain de Beaumont thanked her for picking up right away and acknowledged he probably called at a bad time. He promised not to keep her long. She insisted it was no trouble at all, even as she continued to untangle herself from her luggage, and began to give him a quick thumbnail of her trip. Tonight, Alain had no time for small talk and he stopped her mid-sentence, asking if they could speak of her trip later. He gave the reason for his call as far more urgent, and what he said next sent a shockwave up Suzen's spine.

"Listen carefully. While you were gone, I initiated Plan B."

"What? Why? What on earth happened?"

"A combination of things." Alain knew this conversation was going to be delicate, if not a bit deceitful, and he selected his words carefully. The whole truth was awful and going to be horribly upsetting no matter how he presented it, so he chose to give her the elevator speech. That way he could keep it short and a little vague. He considered throwing in a few alternative facts, too, since he wasn't at liberty to share all the real ones.

He described stumbling across bits and pieces of information that led to a few suspicions and theories. Before he got any further, she interrupted him.

"Wait a minute! Bits and pieces? Suspicions and theories?"

After nearly ten years of working side by side with Will, first as his longtime assistant and now the President of the GeoFibre Foundation, there were no secrets between them, their relationship forged in total trust and great affection for each other.

The same could not be said for her association with his uncle, Alain. They were certainly friendly, and he never failed to show her the utmost respect, but despite all their collaboration she still hadn't the slightest idea who he really was.

What she did know was that he owned a major interest in GeoFibre and was one of two people whose calls she was required to take, immediately. What he did outside GeoFibre, though, was always a little vague. As far as she had been able to glean, he was involved in some sort of advertising, or public relations, or consulting or something, which seemed to require him to disappear for long, unexplained stretches. Since Will never volunteered anything personal about Alain, either, even after Suzen asked him directly, eventually she dropped the subject.

She assumed Alain liked the amount of emotional distance between them, too, and she chalked it up to another of the challenges of living in different hemispheres.

"What in the world is that supposed to mean?" Challenging him might be crossing a line, but Plan B was the name they gave a mission designed to rescue Will, for Heaven's sake. To set it in motion something terrible must have happened, and she wanted to know what it was.

Alain realized it wasn't going to be easy, and he gave her a little more. He said he'd been brought in to consult on a situation developing in New York. There was an unsavory character running around causing a little mischief, and it reminded the authorities of another high-profile guy, nicknamed Le Mauvais.

"Maybe you've heard of him?" he asked offhandedly.

The French language news organizations were the first to dub the assassin Le Mauvais. A vicious thug, he hired himself out to the highest bidder and was notorious for a three-year rampage of brutal execution-style murders of political figures, businessmen and sometimes even celebrities. He soon became as famous as his victims due to another one of his signature moves — avoiding capture — made possible because he remained anonymous. No one had ever seen him or knew what he looked like or even his real name. Alain's team followed his escapades all over Europe, and they nearly caught him at the scene of his final assassination, but he eluded them again. But after that close call, he disappeared, and no further atrocities were ever attributed to him.

"Heard of him? You're talking about that monster who went around breaking peoples' necks? Of course, I've heard of him. He was in the news all the time. I thought he was dead. This is the character you're referring to as unsavory?"

"No, no. Sorry, I didn't mean to mislead you. Nobody thinks the guy they just discovered in New York is the same person. There are too many reasons it is impossible. This is someone new. They believe he's a copycat." He tried to avoid going into any more detail by telling her it was a long, complicated and probably boring story.

"There is nothing remotely boring about a maniac hitman running around in New York," she replied, with more than a tinge of sarcasm. Suddenly, she felt emboldened. "Okay. I'm calm now, and I'm sitting down. Just why are we talking about a hitman?" Her voice broke. "You are scaring me, Alain. What does it have to do with Will and Plan B?"

He waited a few moments to consider his response. It would still only be part of the story, but it would have to suffice, for now. It was plenty bad. He'd get around to telling her the worst part soon enough.

"Apparently, the assassin is no longer running around in New York," he said. "They think he's headed for the Appalachian Trail."

"Oh, my God! Why would he go there? Wait, never mind. Who cares? The important thing is we're getting Will off the trail. We can't have him out there with some killer on the loose," she said. She felt grateful Alain had connections, and as weird as his story was, considered them lucky to learn about the guy in time to do something about it. She regretted leaving the details of that operation to the others. "So, what happens next? Do we need to hire some sort of swat team?"

Alain told her not to worry, that he would take charge of getting Will off the trail.

Before he needed to obfuscate any further she jumped in. "You? Why? What am I missing here?"

"It's part of my skill set," he replied calmly. "Didn't you know?"

She was glad she was sitting down. This had to be one of the most confusing and nerve-wracking conversations of her life. Alain had a lot of explaining to do when this was all over, but for now she wanted to focus on getting Will home safely. She collected herself.

"At least locating him should be easy. We always know exactly where he is."

Alain cleared his throat. "Well, that's actually another problem. We don't."

3

When Will reached the Shady Pines Shelter campsite that night, he was right on schedule. The three-sided structure was built atop a slight slope, and the front of its spacious wooden deck rested on a stack stone wall. An Adirondack-type porch swing on the deck commanded a splendid view of the campsite.

It was tempting to keep things simple, bunk in the shelter and not bother with his tent. It would be his last night on the trail for a while, and he had to be up at first light. Besides, there didn't appear to be anyone else around. A closer look changed his mind. As he neared the top of the steps to the deck he saw a plastic bag full of something and an opened bottle of soda in the middle of the sleeping platform. A hiker had already claimed a spot. Hikers weren't allowed to reserve a whole shelter for themselves. It was always first-come, first-served. In theory, the shelters were large enough to host three or four adults on sleeping bags, though during serious rains and other bad weather more might try to cram in.

Since there were no other hikers around, Will figured whoever owned the bag and the soda probably wouldn't be staying the night since he didn't see any other camping equipment. Still, he couldn't be sure. But he knew one thing: he would not share the space. In fact, there would be no more socializing for him at all. Those were the orders.

Following this new protocol made him feel a little sad, and one more night to enjoy the sounds of owls and birds from his tent seemed to be a better plan. He'd set up his tent, cook up the last of his food and hit the sack.

"Hey, Red Rover."

Again, he was startled from behind. This time, though, he recognized the voice of the hiker shouting up at him. He crossed paths with Streamin a couple of times in the last few days.

"You bunking here tonight? I thought you were going straight on through to Harpers Ferry."

"Hey. Yeah, a slight change of plans," Will shouted back. He remembered suggesting they hang out together a while when they both got to the town. Seeing him reminded him of Streamin's plan to turn around in Georgia and hike all the way back to Maine, known as a 'yo-yo' by the trail intelligentsia. To a non-hiker, the idea of turning around and hiking the whole two thousand miles all over again immediately would undoubtedly sound like lunacy, but in a strange way, Will felt a little envious. When Streamin was out of sight, he went back down the steps to look for a level piece of ground to build a fire.

He thought about how much fun his hike had been and how life-changing. The easy hurdle was the physical one. Being in good shape wasn't enough to hike two thousand miles. This marathon would require stamina, and he trained for it. But there was that other, much larger challenge – his mind. And it didn't just need training. It needed extensive behavior modification. For the twelve waking hours Will hiked every day on the trail, he went without the emails, texts, reports, breaking news and all the rest of the stuff that normally streamed through his brain. It meant going cold turkey from the reliable euphoria a steady bombardment of data delivered. On the trail, he had to score his sensory fix from actual sights and sounds and colors found in nature, not from pixels. It was a transition from a day planner that accounted for every fifteen minutes of his time, to a day planned around two events, sunrise and sunset.

Except for the occasional newspaper he'd run across while shopping for provisions, the only communication with the outside world came through conversations with other hikers. That's how he wanted it. He even designed his powerful watch without a way to browse the Internet, no email client, and no messaging capabilities. He assumed access to any of it would be irresistible. Instead he found the Zen of Hiking much more to his liking.

It was far from the wild and fast ride that brought him there, and his unlikely story — a kid from the obsessively compulsive neat and tidy Swiss culture ends up with a total slob for a college roommate. One semester eleven years ago, Will needed a project for a college applied science class. The assignment was to create a piece of technology from start to finish. It couldn't be a game, and it had to be useful.

William couldn't have been more prepared. In hindsight, he realized his family had been preparing him his whole lifetime. His maternal grandfather was an inventor, and as a young boy Will enjoyed many summer weekends with him. Every Sunday during the formal dinner around the large dining table, the two of them would start a little competition. His grandmother would pick an everyday problem, and after dinner he and his grandfather would head down to the basement to come up with a crazy invention to solve it. In his grandfather's workshop, Will how to use all kinds of hand tools, how to solder and how to build small electronics. Invention became a passion, and he always said it was those days tinkering with his grandfather in the workshop that wired his brain for innovation.

The summer before he started college, an incredible opportunity fell into his lap. A last-minute slot became available at a science camp in Montreux, Switzerland run by some colleagues of his uncle. "Nerd Camp," as he referred to it with his friends only lasted six weeks, and it gave him and eight other boys a chance to learn some advanced coding.

So for him, this college assignment was going to be a snap. The idea came to him in the middle of the night, when his roommate called to ask Will to let him in the front door of their dorm. He was always misplacing his keys, and that night was the third in a row. And there it was — his idea. He called his invention the Doodad. You attached it to something you misplaced often, like a dorm key, and with one click his mobile app would locate the Doodad and the lost item on a map. The first one off the production line went to his roommate, and he gave away a few to his friends. Soon everyone wanted one, or two. Before the end of the semester he was selling hundreds of Doodads online, and the little company he had to form became a case study for another class on writing business plans.

It was shortly after he graduated from college that he and his uncle, Alain, had that flash of genius. *What if his technology could be woven into fabric?* The idea would change their lives forever.

With seed money from his uncle, their vision was no

longer limited to the misplaced car keys of forgetful teenagers. Fabric became labels that could be sewn into clothing. They called their company GeoFibre and through one of his uncle's connections, they won a huge contract with the Department of Defense. Now because their labels were stitched into every single article of clothing in the uniforms throughout all four branches of service, the Pentagon could locate any service member virtually anywhere on the globe. It was then an easy lateral move into the burgeoning logistics industry.

His little company had just made the big pivot, the ubiquitous industry buzzword referring to an important change in direction, and often a big change in revenue. When he studied pivots in one of his classes, he could have no idea that his own company's pivot would end up in Professor O'Shay's curriculum. Or, that a new building to house Entrepreneurial Studies would bear the de Beaumont name.

His mind wandered back again to that same television interview, when the host asked him how he was going to celebrate his success. Would he buy a big house, circle the globe?

"No, no. You've got me all wrong," he insisted.

"Have I?" In fact, she had pointed out several times earlier in the program, much to his annoyance, that his was not the typical rags-to-riches story of the young entrepreneur working on an idea with some friends in his parents' garage.

"I wonder how many people know you were born with a silver spoon in your mouth? An American actress for a mother, a European banker father and a life of privilege on both sides of the Atlantic. Glamorous boarding schools in Switzerland, a fancy college, all that."

"I'm guessing you didn't go to boarding school in Switzerland, did you, Gwen? If you had, I very much doubt you'd portray them as glamorous."

His prep school experience was quite the opposite – Spartan and rigorous. And while he was uncomfortable talking about it, he never denied being born into some advantage. But he cautioned her not to overstate things. He and his family had lead private lives, and he always made a conscious effort not to come across as elitist.

Gwen winked to the studio audience again and suggested that what he referred to as a life of privacy was all relative, considering his former career as a fashion model.

"Well, I'm not sure I'd characterize it as a career. I was just a teenager. And it was only for a couple of seasons."

"So, then I guess your family connections had something to do with getting you the job."

He recounted how he'd been sitting at an outdoor café in Paris with his parents. A woman from a casting agency happened to be at the next table, and his look just happened to be what the fashion industry was looking for. Blah, blah, blah. He promised that was exactly the way it happened.

She chided him about being too modest again and reminded him and her audience that he'd been the face of one of the top luxury brands in the world. The large backdrop screen and studio monitors suddenly filled with full page ads and spreads of William modeling at about age fifteen. The audience members showed their boisterous approval, and after milking the applause, she changed the subject.

"People want to know how you went from fashion model

to business tycoon. She knew he had told the story a million times before, but she and the audience pleaded with him to share it again. That's when he trotted out his story of having to let in his roommate that night, inventing the Doodad, and inheriting his business genes from his dad and creative genes from his mother.

"But let me answer your question of what I am going to do to celebrate." He said he'd grown up in mansions on two continents and had one foot in an airplane since he was an infant, so he didn't need any of those material things. Then he got a little coy. He said he planned to celebrate by doing something he'd always wanted to do, something money couldn't buy. When she got the studio audience to beg for a little clue, he had some fun of his own with them. He arched his eyebrows and spoke in a mysterious voice.

"Let's just say what I'm going to do will be very... low tech."

It seemed eons ago when he offered that clue on television, and he snickered when he recalled she complimented him for his acting ability. Now, standing alone in the middle of the lush woods on a mountain top in the middle of one of the most beautiful stretches of magnificence in the world, that low tech adventure he promised himself would have to be put on hold.

At least until he learned why his life was suddenly in such danger.

4

"Want some help with yer tent?"

It was the same voice that startled him on the trail about an hour earlier. And for the second time this guy seemed to appear out of nowhere, again from behind. Will jumped a bit, embarrassed for being so unnerved. He figured he was still a little skittish from the alert and its inferred danger. But the guy did seem to sneak up on him deliberately. Either way, he decided to keep his cool.

"Oh, hey. Thanks, but nah. I've got one of these crazy simple tents. They practically set themselves up."

"Sweet. Can I watch?"

"Okay, I guess."

Pitching the tent was one of Will's favorite parts of setting up camp because it was so insanely easy. All wrapped up, his tent measured only about a yard long and a few inches around. Finding it too frustrating to fit it back in the matching bag it came in every morning, he ditched it long ago. Another hiker he met along the way said the bag would be perfect for something she needed, so he gave it to her. That's the way it worked on the trail. Things got recycled among hikers. Now one bungee cord sufficed to hold everything together.

In the meantime he needed to distance himself from the guy standing next to him. Will knew he couldn't be the reason for the warning. The timing didn't fit. Whatever he had to worry about was still ten hours away. Even so, he decided as soon as he finished showing him how the tent worked, he would establish some boundaries. This part of the protocol was unmistakably clear — *After receiving an alert, don't engage with anyone.*

What annoyed him was the guy's habit of standing so close.

"Like I said, there's really nothing to it." Will took several steps to one side to create some space between them. "Watch this." He pulled up on a cord and the bundle began to unpack itself and become a tent. While he needed to use his hands to help along some of the more stubborn sections, the whole process took less than a minute.

"Sweet," said the hiker, stepping into his space again. Will continued the dance and retreated several more paces.

"How does it go back down?"

"It's easy. You just pull off these top hubs and straighten out the legs. It comes down just as fast." Will regretted letting himself be drawn into this conversation.

"Sweet!" The hiker paused. "Show me."

Will found that weird, and he realized he absolutely needed to disengage from this guy. While not wanting to be a jerk, he was prepared to take more serious measures. If this was indeed the hiker with only the little plastic bag and the soda up in the shelter, he likely wouldn't be spending the night. Will thought maybe he'd leave soon, anyway.

"No, I don't think so. If you're up early enough tomorrow you can watch me take it down then."

"I'm gonna get me one of them tents," mumbled the newcomer.

"They're pretty cheap." Will felt glad his American mother made him spend so many summers in the States. Like his uncle, he'd developed a flawless American accent at a young age. It contrasted so sharply with discourse of the newcomer, they might as well have been speaking different languages. He avoided eye contact as he spoke. "You can get them online," he mumbled. He wanted to kick himself for continuing the conversation.

The hiker's expression went blank. "Online?" he asked.

Will considered the unlikelihood of a so-called tech superstar running into one of the thirteen percent of American adults who still didn't use the Internet. And a young guy, at that. Will had a lot on his mind, and what he needed now was to eat and squeeze in what little sleep he could within the short time frame left. He deliberately turned his back on the guy, began to gather firewood and started to organize his cooking gear.

The strategy worked. Without saying another word the hiker crossed back over the clearing and climbed the steps up to the shelter's front deck, making it clear that he owned the stuff up there. He plopped down on the wooden porch swing, and it gave a loud creak in resistance. It cried out louder when he leaned back on it. Out of the corner of his eye, Will watched him start to swing, using his right foot against the deck floor to push the swing back. Then, almost childlike, he grabbed onto the chains, leaned back and lifted both legs into the air for the ride forward. Then he pushed the swing back with his foot again. The links in the chain ground and squeaked with each pass. Back and forth. Steady rhythm. Squeak, squeak. And as he swung, he stared at Will, watching him work.

"They call you Red Rover," the guy called over after a short while. He was still swinging on the platform, but he called loud enough for Will to hear. His delivery sounded flat, without affect.

As unnerving as it was, Will decided to put a positive spin on it. After all, the little exchange would make a nice chapter in the book he planned to write about his adventures. It would scare the crap out of almost anybody. In the meantime, Will determined to ignore him. Fortunately, he didn't need to look at him to know he was still swinging. The links of the swing's chains were still making a creaking noise. He was probably still staring, too, but Will felt glad at least he was over there.

With the weirdo up on the shelter deck, Will could refocus on fixing his last supper on the trail. It was going to be a huge one, too, because he had just done a little shopping the day before, and he wanted to use everything up. It would be easy to restock with fresh provisions back in Harpers Ferry when he could resume the hike. That was, after he resolved a problem so potentially serious they made him take a break.

Right now, though, he was comfortable sitting on the log facing the fire. His pasta was boiling in a pot, while he quietly stirred garlic and onions around in his pan. Something the family cook told him one day when he was a young boy hanging around in the kitchen brought a smile to his face. "Whatever you're going to cook, always start by sautéing some onions."

The sizzle and aroma never failed to elevate his mood, and his mind began to wander back to why he was being taken off the trail. It couldn't be a business issue, because his uncle had the authority to act on Will's behalf. Besides, he was in complete support of Will's Appalachian Trail dream, and Will knew he would never attempt to interrupt it. It had to be something else, something serious enough to trigger Plan B. But what?

The onions were ready and he took them off the fire to wait for the pasta to finish cooking. He decided to use the time to make the day's entry in his journal. It would be just enough time, and he knew it would help him take his mind off the intruder. For two and a half months he'd practiced focusing on the moment, and now, after all that training, his brain was starting to fill with thoughts and chatter again. He forced himself to return to the present — to the journal. Soon he was alone again on the log enjoying the peaceful quiet of the wilderness.

The quiet? He stopped writing. He sensed something wasn't right, but wasn't sure just what. He remained motionless and listened. Was it an animal? No, he hadn't heard anything. Yes, that's what it was. There was nothing to hear. What happened to the squeaking of the chains? How long ago did it stop? He checked the swing. It was empty and motionless, so it had been a little while, anyway. He stared all around. No sign of the guy. Maybe he finally left. Will sure hoped so. All the same, not knowing sent a little tingle up his spine.

5

In preparation for his hike the guys at Will's lab sewed GeoFibre labels onto some of his clothing and gear, so his New York office could track their valuable boss. His exact location bounced off satellites from the labels twenty-four-seven. It synthesized with elevation, speed, rest times and other data and streamed to a huge digital 3D map of the entire two thousand mile Appalachian Trail. The map occupied the length of one whole wall of what had been a large conference room situated between Suzen's office and Will's. Because of its location, the moment by moment updates to the arrays and overlays of continually flashing lights and numbers would dazzle only a few privileged pairs of eyes. Knowledge of Will's movement and location was to be kept under wraps.

In addition to providing his exact whereabouts, all that data would come in handy later for the memoir he planned to pen, and the location and weather data collected in the office would be invaluable in refreshing his memory. Another part of the low-tech adventure was keeping an actual diary. Hand-written. Every night without fail, before going to sleep, Will wrote an entry. He found it a little hard at first, but not from a lack of discipline, because part of the rigor of his boarding school experience included keeping a journal. While he still maintained the routine, the mechanics had changed since those early days. Prior to the hike he used a speech to text app which made it all so simple. The app converted his voice to text, all of it date-stamped and stored in one cloud or another. The real challenge he faced on the trail was reverting to the original method — writing with an actual pen in a real notebook.

It wasn't the only manual record of his trip being kept. Will's uncle Alain was more comfortable with a human interface as an extra safeguard in what would otherwise be a data-driven procedure. In this case, an actual human from upper level management was to enter his coordinates each day in a physical notebook. That same person then manually would send an encrypted email alert each day to Alain and Suzen, pinpointing Will's exact location. By logging it at the same time every day, this person would be able to check it against the proposed itinerary. They could interpret the data and know immediately if anything seemed abnormal. One day they noticed Will backtracking north for twenty-four hours. The following day, when he'd turned around and headed south again, another notation was made. Naturally, they realized a trip of over two thousand miles would be subject to some variation, but it gave everyone a pretty good idea where he should be at any time. Will had stuck to his plan. In fact, he was ahead of schedule.

6

"What do you mean, we don't know where he is?" Suzen's response was quick and sharp.

"The email alerts giving his location stopped coming a week ago. Didn't you notice?"

There followed a long silence as she scrolled frantically through the emails on her phone. "What? Wait, here it is, the last one. It's dated the day before I left the country."

"Yes, it was the last one I received, too."

She told him not to worry and added that Dillon, the office manager, promised to keep an eye on Will. She promised to call him and get a handle on things first thing in the morning. Alain said he called their New York office to find out why, and he was alarmed that no one either picked up the phone or returned his call. Ever. That whole day or the next. He wondered if anyone was in the office at all.

"That's when I knew something was very wrong, and it was time for Plan B.

"My god. I feel sick. I'm on my way to the office!" She snapped off the lights, grabbed her purse and bolted out of her apartment.

"Oh, and there's something else," Alain added. "I wanted you to know I'm here."

Surprised, she asked if he wanted to meet her at the office.

"No, I don't mean in New York. I meant I'm here, in the field."

"In the field?" His ability to be vague no longer surprised her.

"Yes, Harpers Ferry, West Virginia. I've been here a few weeks."

7

Alain hung up the phone, wishing he could have told Suzen everything he wanted to. Not being able to share much about his former day job was one of the tradeoffs in his line of work, and it contributed to his chronic sense of detachment and loneliness. This time, though, it felt like more than that. In this case, he was afraid if Suzen knew too much it could put her at risk. And how could he tell her the other part? It was difficult enough for him to process.

Following the sudden and enormous financial success of their company, he and Will established the GeoFibre Foundation with grand plans for doing good works all over the world. They also imagined it would be a vehicle for them to spend more time together. Alain contributed his time and expertise as an advisor, and in two short years the Foundation became successful and sustainable, and working together with Will they set many of those grand plans in motion. But as fulfilling as it was, Alain had to face facts. He missed the thrills of his old job. Sometimes so badly he felt he'd robbed his core of its very lifeblood.

Major M's offer came to him on a day two months earlier, the only message to populate an old email address Alain still maintained and rarely used. The curious salad of letters would have looked like spam to anyone else, but Alain de Beaumont recognized the gobbledygook. And the encrypted message from his former colleague was clear:

Lots of chatter on the Dark Web. Le Mauvais possibly in New York. Want in?

It asked Alain to use his old secured phone line to call a former colleague, and while the email did not specify the call was urgent, it didn't have to. It was Major M, a man who was an expert at pushing other people's buttons. He knew Alain liked nothing more than following a fresh scent down a trail, and this time it only took one whiff. Encrypted messages, secured lines, chasing villains again. Alain was a young fifty-five, and he smelled adventure, and it was intoxicating. This time it came with the added element of unfinished business.

Alain made the call. It began with each accusing the other of failing to keep up the relationship, but it didn't take long for the conversation between two old friends to fall into comfortable rhythms. Major M said he was now splitting his time between his home operation in Lyon and now Singapore, the location of Interpol's new Global Complex, and he bragged a bit about Interpol's revised mission of boosting cybersecurity and countering cybercrime. The two men knew all too well that the glamour associated with a career as an Interpol agent did not exist outside the world of spy novels, and the hope was that this enhanced mission would burnish the organization's standing within law enforcement organizations everywhere.

He added how the public-facing makeover provided even better cover for the super-secret agency he ran buried deep within it. Extraordinary new backdoor funding for their covert operation came willingly from the American, British, and European intelligence services, who were all too eager for a way to collaborate on selective and sensitive missions without leaving any traces of involvement by their own spy organizations. Major M was responsible for conceiving of the idea to hide his elite group in plain sight. Not only did Interpol provide credentials, its dazzling new intelligence gathering technology was available to all of them. He suggested that even Alain would be impressed at the dramatic improvements, since he took his leave of absence.

"I don't know why I'm blustering on. I've heard your setup at GeoFibre might possibly rival ours."

"Oh, stop it! Yes, it is all very slick, but you know GeoFibre's investments in technology were necessary for our current tracking operations."

Major M ribbed Alain about being a corporate bigwig and the de Beaumonts being in the news all the time. Though he was officially Chairman of GeoFibre, Alain spent most of his time and focus on its charitable foundation. And his friend was right. Their initiatives were well-reported as the outreach of the Foundation continued to touch thousands of lives around the world.

"Okay, enough of all that." They both knew it wasn't a social call, and Alain was eager to get to the point. "You mentioned Le Mauvais. He's been on my mind lately. Truth be told, I never really stopped thinking about him. So, what do you have in mind. I'm all ears."

Major M started with a confession. He admitted it was a bit of an exaggeration to suggest that Alain's old friend, Le Mauvais was currently in New York. It was meant to attract Alain's attention. So was referring to him as his old friend.

Nemesis was more like it, and he hoped Alain would see the job as an opportunity for vindication.

Shortly after he completed his final execution, Interpol connected the dots of some suspicious transfers of funds with airline manifests and determined the thug was doing his hiding in Thailand. About eighteen months earlier a local operative was confident she identified him in Bangkok, getting off a bus returning from Chiang Mai. Awkward eye contact between them set off another quick string of events, and in seconds, Le Mauvais rounded a corner and disappeared. Though he was never seen again, they'd kept a strict eye on the place ever since, and with all the resources they put to that effort, his leaving the country without their knowledge would have been next to impossible. Even if he did, re-entering the States would have triggered multiple alerts, because in addition to being on any number of terrorist lists, thanks to Alain, there was a photograph at every passport control in the free world.

For though Alain never succeeded in capturing the man, he did capture his face. One evening a routine sting operation set up to expose a money-laundering scheme, involving a Russian diplomat and an American real estate mogul, became more complicated. When the group showed up for the sting at that Madrid hotel, they were very surprised to find the American dead in his room. And while Le Mauvais had left without a trace, Alain's hidden camera managed to take the only snapshot they ever had of him. His photos were posted and distributed physically everywhere, and they went as viral as was possible in those early stages of social media. The photo was a bit blurry, but apparently Le Mauvais thought it was a close enough likeness, that it spooked him into hiding. Ironically, instead of being useful in his apprehension, because of the photo, they lost him forever.

Major M asked if Alain had read the news about the recent death of a Danish journalist in New York City. Everyone had seen it, of course; it was a breaking news headline all over the world, because the woman was about to reveal massive, but still alleged election tampering by a foreign government.

"I didn't follow it closely, but didn't she die from some complication or another from a previous illness?"

"Ha! How soon you forget. I'll give you the exact quote." He recited it from the obituary. "She died in her sleep after fighting a tough illness — an illness she'd kept even from her family."

"Uh, oh. I know what that means." He'd invented the same line a long time ago to explain away another of Le Mauvais' high-profile executions.

Because the technique used to execute the journalist was identical, his group was asked to step in. It didn't take long for him to be convinced what they were dealing with now was a darned good copycat running loose in New York.

"We think if we catch him, we can connect the dots to our old friend. Are you ready to end this ill-advised leave of absence?"

"I can start this afternoon," Alain jested.

They decided he would work from New York. Major M would reactivate his security clearance and send in a team to do a sweep of Alain's West Village row house on Eleventh Street and update his electronics. In a few days he could be up and running and would know as much as they did about the copycat's movements. Alain felt exhilarated. He would reassign his duties at the Foundation and tidy up a few personal things and leave for New York in a week or so.

The euphoria was short-lived, though, when the next day he got another call from Major M.

"Are you going to renege on your offer already?"

This time Major M was less chatty. Alain recognized it as his serious business voice. He said he'd called to ask how Alain's nephew, William François, was doing on his famous hike. Major M gave up trying to choose between William or François long ago and settled on using both names together.

Famous hike? His question caught Alain off guard. He and the powers that be at GeoFibre had taken great pains to keep Will's plans private. The only clue Will ever gave was to that insistent interviewer, and all he told her was that he was going to do something very low tech.

"All right, now you've got me worried," said Alain. "Why would you be watching him?"

"Well, we're not... really. But you must know everyone kind of keeps an eye on him. William François and GeoFibre are important to the world. The only thing we know is that he's hiking the Appalachian Trail and approximately where and when he entered. Since he started in Maine, we assume he's hiking the whole enchilada."

"Yes, fine, you're right, of course, but remind me, why are we talking about him at all?"

Alain's heart sank when Major M told him theory about the copycat had grown some legs, and that new chatter they were following suggested that a de Beaumont might be his target.

His voice cracked. "But why François? He has no enemies."

"But you do. I'm sorry, friend. But unless you are speaking to me from the Appalachian Trail, the only other de Beaumont the target can be is your nephew. And a reasonable explanation would be..."

Alain didn't hear Major M finish his sentence. He knew the other explanation...revenge. "So, Le Mauvais is behind this after all."

"Listen, Alain, like I said, we have him contained. I'm sure we both can think of several guys who would like to get some payback from you."

"But how would anyone know François is hiking the trail? That's been a closely guarded secret."

"I'm afraid I can't answer that."

"What's the time frame? Do I need to pull him off the trail now?"

"Oh, there's no need to spoil his fun yet." He tried to reassure Alain that what they picked up was still preliminary. Like so many messages they intercepted, it could just as easily end up being nothing at all. "You know how these things go."

Just in case it did develop into something more serious, Major M wanted a rescue plan in place. He acknowledged it would be a significant challenge, given the over two-thousand-mile-long trail. "Do you think you could work up a few scenarios? You were always better at that than I was."

"We're way ahead of you," interjected Alain. He explained how they always knew his exact location, because unlike Major M's organization, Alain and GeoFibre were tracking him twenty-four-seven. Furthermore, since François had been sticking to a detailed itinerary, should the time come to pull him off they would only need to concern themselves with a small section of the trail. "Who do you have in mind to run the op?"

Under the circumstances, Major M elected not to skirt around the issue, and instead he went straight with the offer. "You'd have all the resources you'd need, and the agency would do the heavy lifting."

With all the manpower, the fleets of surveillance drones and the agency's other equipment at his disposal, Alain felt relieved. The contingency plans he'd developed all required additional personnel and assets. Now, he could execute any of his scenarios at a moment's notice. Given those advantages, a rescue seemed easy to accomplish.

And even though it was still experimental, he had incorporated Plan B into each one. It would be a real-time opportunity to test some of their advanced nanotechnology.

"I know he's been like a son to you."

Alain anticipated Major M's question and took the offense. "I know what you're going to ask, and we both know you have to ask it. Yes, of course it's going to be personal. I can't imagine anything more personal. I believe that when my brother died, he left me François as his parting gift, and he has become the most important person in my life. You want my assurance that it won't cloud my thinking."

"So, will it? Please tell me it won't."

Major M didn't need to remind him about the incident in Cairo, when Alain misinterpreted the intentions of a woman and ended up nearly compromising the entire mission. He pushed the memory away. "And don't bring up Egypt. I was much younger when I allowed that lapse in judgement. You know I can compartmentalize my emotions."

He felt confident and added that he wanted complete control over the operation. If that was acceptable he'd take a GeoFibre jet and leave Geneva for the States the next day.

"I'm not worried at all," said Major M. "We all know you could rescue your nephew with your hands tied behind your back."

But Major M had another shoe to drop. In exchange for providing manpower and resources, the mission would need a second outcome – Alain would have to bring in the new hitman.

The stipulation was not entirely unexpected, but it would add significantly to the difficulty, and to the risk. He and Major M had a lifetime of experience with covert rescue operations in much more remote areas in the world, and still, he knew the second part would be far more difficult. It didn't help that the agency had few details and no description of him.

It took no time at all for Alain to get ready. He always had a bag packed for business, and he'd pick up whatever else he needed when he got there. And then, there was the other bag. He'd been away from the agency for two years, but he still clung to it, keeping it ready even though he didn't expect to need it again. It reminded him of having to dispose of the personal effects of his spouse. Parting with some things was just plain hard.

Like so many scenarios he'd put together before, this one would reliably be in a state of flux. Extracting a lost person from the wilderness was tricky enough. In this case, the target would be moving. Targets, technically speaking. His nephew was the easy one. The team would know what he looked like, and he'd be expecting a rescue. Not knowing much about the assassin complicated matters. All they knew about him was that William François was his target.

And this time there would be a third wrinkle. He would have to accomplish both aspects of the mission while attracting as little attention as possible. Major M had given another caveat. Officially closing off the trail until they finished wasn't an option. With all the hikers crisscrossing parts of it at any given time news would spread quickly, and not only could that jeopardize the mission, it would be a public relations nightmare for the entire Appalachian Trail. His head spun.

He'd had been staring out the window at the vast ocean beneath him for about an hour, wondering who was behind all this and how they knew about the hike, when an idea came to him. It was perhaps a little far-fetched, but he gave a directive to the pilot anyway. In seconds the plane banked and a new flight plan was posted.

Several hours later when the jet's descent awakened him, he saw the sprawling Suvarnabhumi airport just below. As much as he loved the city, this time he only would see one person and wouldn't be staying more than a few hours. Of course, that would depend completely on traffic. Bangkok was notorious for its gridlock.

He was glad his regular driver would be waiting. He really knew how to get around the city and where to get the best noodles. He knew a lot of other secrets, too.

8

At just after eleven in the evening Suzen entered the GeoFibre Foundation on Eighth Avenue in Times Square, and one quick look around was enough to put her mind at ease. The office was far from its normal pristine condition, but not a complete mess. A stack of unopened mail and a few packages lay piled on the floor in the reception area. Not too bad, for being closed for a week.

Will's love of order could be seen reflected in the office. He expected every employee to walk the talk as well. He got some of that passion from his American side. 'A place for everything, and everything in its place,' was a line his maternal grandparents would often repeat. Will even engraved it on a plaque hanging prominently on the wall above the sink in the staff kitchen, and true to form, the place was pristine. She'd have to find her answers elsewhere.

No matter how fast their company jet traveled and how much the luxury could minimize the effects of jet lag, trips like these between hemispheres left her both completely exhausted and simultaneously wide awake. After being away for a week she looked forward to spending the night in her own bed, not on the sofa in her office.

Will always referred to Suzen as his "right hand arm," an expression the press loved to repeat. She'd been with him from the start and had no traditional training. But she was smart, a quick study and intuitive. As the company grew, she'd grown with it, and that meant fast, because the company was only about ten years old. He trusted her with everything, and she'd earned it. Besides, she learned to speak decent French.

It was dark and silent except for the occasional gentle whirring sound of some electronic thingamajig or another cycling on and off. Some of her staff said they were uncomfortable alone there at night, but it never felt creepy to her. She felt glad they kept the original office space when they split off the Foundation from the rest of GeoFibre. She and Will spent so many crazy late nights there in those frantic early days when it was an emerging startup. This office felt like her second home, and tonight she was particularly nostalgic.

She carried her coffee into her suite. The foundation operated with a relatively small staff, and she and Will were the only ones to have private offices. There were a few dedicated work spaces, but administrative support came from the main company on the floor below. Everyone else, though, either worked from home, on the road, or they came in to share the few workspace 'hotels' scattered throughout the suite. Such was the current trend in office design. A large conference room occupied the space between her suite and Will's, accessible from each of their offices. For the duration of Will's hike that space served as the map room.

She didn't bother turning on the lights in her office. Instead, she headed directly for her sofa. She'd delve into the issue of why the alerts weren't going out in a minute. In the meantime, the cool leather felt soothing on the back of her neck. Sinking in deeper, she began to relax. She was sleepier now than an hour ago when she told Alain she would head right over. Her mind started to wander a bit and slowly her eyelids began to droop. She knew if she wasn't careful she would nod off, and to prevent that adjusted her body and sat up straight. Still, the soft leather and the quiet darkness felt overpowering, and her body sagged with fatigue. In a few short moments, she was out.

Clunk. Her chin struck her chest when her head fell, and she jerked upright. Her hand groped in the dark on the side sofa table and found her coffee mug. Aware of what a close call it had been she took a long slug. Caffeine reliably kept her from falling asleep, and she knew it was safe to lean back while it kicked in. She began to gather her thoughts and mentally set some priorities. There was so much to do, and she needed to be at the top of her game.

Glancing at the glass wall between her office and the map room she thought about Will, and hoped his uncle Alain was being overly dramatic and unnecessarily worried. She clung to the part where Alain said the threat wasn't definite. He did say that, didn't he?

It was peaceful sitting there alone. Like the rest of the office, it was pitch black and soothing. She closed her eyes again and tried to focus on positive thoughts. Suddenly she sat up again. Dark? Soothing? Something was very wrong. It should not be pitch black in the map room. Where were the flashing lights and data scrawls? She leaped to her feet, almost spilling her coffee, and dashed across her office into the black conference room. She switched on the lights and took a quick look around. Then she picked up the leather bound alert log and raced back to her office. Her first call went to GeoFibre's Chief Technology Officer. It was a lucky break she caught him still working on another floor. Soon after they arrived she made the second call. To Alain.

Suzen shared with him what the engineers told her. The system was disabled, with no satellite feeds for at least several days. They told her it was a real mess and the result of sabotage. It would take them a while to figure out what happened, and even longer to get it back up and running. Maybe for as long as several days. She did feel gratified to report none of the GeoFibre mainframes around the world were affected.

"It looks like the damage was confined here, so at least that's a relief," she added trying to sound upbeat. He heard a muffled sound, and she said, "Excuse me for a minute, please, Alain."

In fifteen seconds she was back, with a message from her team. "They said they can fix it, Alain. They said there is no reason to worry."

"I wish I shared your optimism," he said.

He hated to throw his wet blanket on her one piece of good news, but he realized now was the moment to tell her the truth – that Will was the assassin's target. He needed her help, and to get it, he needed to gain her trust.

He decided to drop the bomb. Predictably, she didn't take it well.

9

"I passed you on the trail," said the hiker from behind.

Will nearly jumped out of his skin. It had been a while since he'd noticed the empty swing. He thought he left. At least he hoped he left. Now, there he was, standing right behind him. This time he felt positive he intentionally sneaked up on him. On purpose.

"I passed you on the trail," he repeated.

Will pretended he hadn't noticed him, and looked straight into the fire when he responded, "Oh, was that you?"

"Maybe," teased the hiker.

A loud hissing sound came from the pot where the water had boiled away, and the noodles were beginning to burn. Will was so focused on not interacting, he hadn't paid attention to what he was doing – cooking. He pulled the pot off the fire and dumped in some water from his canteen and managed to save his meal. "I guess dinner's ready," he mumbled.

"Can I have some?"

Will tried another tactic. He ignored him. *At least this is going to taste good*, he thought, as he strained the noodles with his fork and mixed in the vegetables.

The hiker pointed at the food and asked him again, this time more forcefully. Since ignoring the guy didn't work, Will decided the best he could do was not to provoke him.

"Um, sure, I guess. It's just pasta. I cooked way too much anyway. Got a bowl?"

"Nope."

"Well, okay. Um. Here, you can use mine." He filled his bowl for the guy. Will would eat his own directly out of the pot.

"You got sumthin' to eat this with?"

Will reluctantly handed over his only fork.

It was obvious by now that the guy wasn't a real hiker. Completely unequipped with the basics, there he was on the trail at night. His continued presence created agitation and Will found it difficult to eat with the mindfulness he'd developed over the past months. Instead, he wolfed down his food. Knowing he couldn't show his anxiety he decided to reverse his strategy completely. He'd befriend the guy.

"Hey, friend, if we are going to be neighbors, we should at least know each other's name. For some reason you know mine, ha-ha, but I don't know yours."

The guy looked up and grinned. "Yeah, you're Red Rover." He inched down the log a little closer to Will and resumed eating. This time it was more than just an invasion of his personal space. It was getting seriously creepy. Will could hear his own heart beating.

He stood up abruptly and announced he was going to clean up and turn in. He told the guy he would fill his canteen from the water pump just down the path behind the shelter. Then he grabbed his backpack and left. It was a ploy. His canteen had plenty of water for the short trip to the pickup site in the morning.

What he wanted to do was change the scene, the story an excuse to leave. He thought if he stayed out of sight long enough the creep would lose interest and be gone by the time Will went back.

He forced himself to stand behind the shelter and killed time by staring at his watch. After about ten minutes he came back to the clearing, hoping to have the campfire to himself. He shuddered when he saw what was waiting for him. Not only was the guy still sitting at the fire but he was wearing Will's coat.

"Cold," the hiker said with a smile, as though that one word would explain everything.

"Hey, man. That, I'm afraid you can't have. It's the only one I've got, and I'm going to need it myself tonight."

He used a guy-to-guy voice. It wasn't threatening, just firm.

"Cold," the hiker repeated, this time with his arms folded across his chest, daring Will to take it from him.

"Yeah, I'm cold too. So, would you hand it over now, please?"

Silence. It was the sound of a standoff. Then Will had another idea. "I've something else to keep you warm. Yeah," he said as he produced a tiny space blanket from an outer pocket of his pack. "You are going to love this."

The guy's eyes lit up, and he grabbed the little plastic pouch.

"Good. Glad, you like it. I'll trade you."

There was an awkward silence as the hiker tore open the pouch. When he finished unfolding the blanket, he draped it over his shoulders, right on top of his new jacket.

Will stared at him in disbelief. "You know, go ahead and keep the jacket. No need to give it back. Okay?"

"I want your backpack, too."

Will pointed toward the shelter. "Hey, friend...look. I'm not sure where you are going with this, but I think it's time you went back to your spot over there."

"I don't think so," came the quiet response. Then it got tougher and louder. "Sit back down!" he yelled.

A blinding light reflecting from a shiny object in the guy's lap pierced Will's eyes. The light source was the campfire, and the shiny object was the blade of Will's hunting knife, now in the hiker's hands. The guy rotated it back and forth, focusing the reflection across Will's face.

His own knife looked a lot more menacing in the other guy's hands, and he looked like he knew how to use it. Will hoped robbery was all the guy had in mind. They were about the same size, but Will could tell he was no match for him. He backed down immediately. "Look, buddy. There's no need to get rough here. What do you want from me? You want my backpack? Take it. It's yours."

The guy reached over and grabbed the straps. Before he released the pack, Will remembered it still held a large wad of cash, and he offered to split it with him. The guy ignored him and pulled the pack forcibly from Will, and once in his possession hugged it tight like a child with a toy he didn't want to share.

"Okay, then. Well, that's settled." Will pretended to yawn. "Why don't we both just turn in now?"

It turned out the guy wanted his tent and the rest of his gear. While he was at it, he wanted his sweater. Pulling it off exposed his watch, and the guy's eyes brightened at the very sight of it. Will knew he would have to cooperate and give him whatever he wanted if he wanted to get out of there alive.

"I hope you'll at least let me keep my pants," he stammered.

"Yeah."

The hiker put the knife in his mouth while he bound Will's hands together. He used Will's own bungee cords. After he was satisfied he tied Will tightly enough, he focused his attention on his newest toy, the watch. He'd never seen anything like it before. Dials, icons and buttons appeared out of nowhere just by grazing the screen with a finger. He poked at it here and there without a clue of what he was doing. Or what the watch could do, for that matter.

"Want me show you how to use it? It can do some pretty neat tricks."

"Okay, but don't try anything." He pointed to the knife which was now at his side.

"There's not much I can do like this." Will lifted his bound hands up from his lap to convey his helpless expression. It was dark and cool up there in the mountains. He was only wearing a long-sleeved T-shirt now, and the half of his body not facing the fire was starting to get cold. The guy passed the watch back to him. Navigating was awkward at first with his wrists tied together, but he could do well enough using only his thumbs. He pushed buttons, activating counters and sweep hands to demonstrate some of the features. One of the icons brought up a map.

"See where this red dot is blinking?" he said tilting the watch face in the guy's direction. "That's where we are right now." It didn't seem to interest him. In fact, none of the functions seemed to keep his attention, and Will was afraid of losing him. Then he had an idea. With a few more finger swipes across the screen, he pulled up a game. He explained that in the game, pumpkins with big teeth chased a farmer around his farm. The longer you could keep him from getting bitten, the more pumpkins appeared and the harder it got. Will played it with his thumbs, and the guy was fascinated, hypnotized even. He leaned in for a better look.

Will knew he was physically no match for the guy, so his only chance was to catch him by surprise. Now that Will was convinced the guy was completely intrigued, he asked him if he wanted to take a crack at it. He nodded back and they made the handover. As soon as it left Will's hands, the watch's security system let out a high-pitched SCREECH, and the piercing sound took the guy completely by surprise. He squeezed his eyes shut and covered his ears with both hands, making him completely unprepared for what was to come.

Tied together at his wrist, Will's hands made a powerful weapon, and he gave the hiker guy a sharp uppercut to his chin. Then he plowed his fists into the guy's nose a couple of times. He jumped to his feet and dealt several hard blows to the back of his head and the guy keeled over. His head landed near the fire.

With the guy down, Will looked around in the dark for the knife so he could cut the binding on his wrists. First things, first. But it wasn't enough time. The man with no name was down and a little dazed, but not out of commission. And it wasn't the constant wailing of the watch's alarm that made him suddenly bolt upright but his hair getting singed which revived him.

He was still on the ground, though, and that was enough of an advantage for Will to get a head start. He took off in the dark as fast as he could toward the woods. He wasn't sure where he was going, and he didn't care.

The guy extinguished the burning hairs with a few slaps to his head and scrambled to his feet. It was dark, but he could see Will in the distance, and he still had the knife in his hand. Although a little wobbly throwing one was second nature, and he took aim. Will slowed and turned to look back, just as the guy released the weapon. He spun around, but not in time. The knife stung when it hit, and Will went down.

The guy's nose was bleeding, his head still hurt, and now LED lights on the watch started flashing to add to the cacophony. It drove him crazy, and desperate to shut it all off and make the noise go away he fumbled and fiddled with the buttons. Frantic, he was about to toss the trouble-making watch into the fire when it suddenly went silent.

His face relaxed as the screen returned to its Home Page, and then he saw it — the icon for *Pumpkin Menace*. He double clicked on it the way he'd seen Red Rover do, and the controls came into view.

Snap. The sound came from somewhere off in the woods. He stood up and looked around. It had to be an animal; it couldn't be a human. There hadn't been any other hikers out there except Red Rover, and he just took care of him. He hadn't meant to kill him, of course, but even above all the noise coming from the watch, he'd heard the howl, and knew he hit his mark. He only wanted the guy's stuff. Earlier in the day he heard another hiker say Red Rover's equipment was expensive, and he always needed money. And so what if he was dead? Nobody would link him to it. It wasn't likely any more hikers would pass by, either. It was too late, and too dark.

His face lit up, because the watch and the game were all his now, and he had all the time in the world. He sat down back down on the log and started playing. In no time, he was captivated.

10

With the computer in the New York office still compromised, they could no longer track his GeoFibre labels, so Alain was in the field to find his nephew the old-fashioned way. Alain was dressed in black, from head to toe. As a boy he dreamed of being a Ninja warrior, not in small part because of the look. He was crazy about the outfit. While this night he was not nearly as young nor as skinny as the comic book character, he knew he was as close as he would ever be. He felt confident in his rescue plan, and he knew he personally brought his A game. Plan B had been set in motion, and teams were in place at the right locations. Why then, he wondered, did he have such a terrible feeling in his gut?

It made the most sense for him to begin looking at the campsite, because according to the master itinerary François planned to overnight there. It also wasn't far from the spot where he'd returned the Plan B signal. That was suspect, though. The delay in the ping had been considerable, and the technicians in Switzerland could only give their best estimate as to when and where Will sent it.

Alain had his own Plan B. If he didn't find François at the campsite he hoped at least to find clues to where he might be.

It was pitch black when he emerged from the woods and entered the clearing. Through night goggles he'd been watching the area for about twenty minutes. Watching and listening. There had been no activity at all since he arrived, a good sign. It meant part of his larger plan, the deployment of a batch of fake rangers up and down the trail to "encourage" hikers to exit at Harpers Ferry was working. They concocted a story about a large family of aggressive bears in the immediate area, and they called it a serious safety issue. They wanted the hikers to feel they were leaving the trail voluntarily, and they sweetened the pot by offering to put everyone up at no charge in hostels and hotels in town, insisting it would be very temporary. If hikers resisted departing the trail, the fake rangers were told to ratchet up the tall tale enough to where it finally would scare them into compliance. They were primed with several progressively frightening scenarios they could recite, and if that still didn't work, they were instructed to use whatever means they needed. Fortunately, those means had not been necessary.

As he approached the glowing remnants of the campfire it was hard not to notice one amber light apart from the others, from a spot just outside the ring of ashes. At first, he thought it might be just another ember, but the color was distinctly different, and the light pulsed on and off in a regular pattern. He could tell the thing was hand-made and resembled an old television remote with one button... and connected earbuds. Whatever it was, it sat far enough away from the fire to avoid heat damage. Though the plastic earbud wires were melted in places, the body of the device was not charred or even warm. There in the dark, Alain had no way of knowing if this gizmo was related in any way to the assassin, or just the property of a random hiker, but whatever it was he'd get it checked out right away. If it wasn't damaged by the heat he knew his guys would be able to identify its purpose.

It was time to examine the rest of the objects near the fire. There were the obvious ones. Cooking utensils were organized in front of one of the log seats, no doubt the place where the camper was sitting. It looked like the remains of some type of pasta in the cook pot. There was a bowl and a spoon left unwashed, as well. If the owner left, they'd gone without taking their cook set with them, which seemed unlikely. Washed or unwashed, he felt confident his nephew would never have left dishes lying around. It would have been considered litter, and like the entire Swiss population, litter appalled him.

As he poked around the remaining embers he felt discouraged. The evidence was mounting to suggest it wasn't Will's campsite. He noticed a canteen lying on the ground next to the log, and when he picked it up, judged it to be at least half full. That added another layer to the mystery. Considering there was plenty of water, why would the person have left without extinguishing the fire? Will would certainly never have done that. Unless he was in a big hurry.

It had to be someone else's stuff and campsite. Someone irresponsible, for sure. Alain had been sitting and staring at the ashes, when he developed a cramp in his legs. He rearranged his position, and one of his boots dragged against something on the ground, half-covered with dirt and leaves. When he dusted it off he recognized the dark brown leather bound journal he'd given Will to use on his trip. The irony was not lost on him, that his parting gift to Will was now Will's parting gift to him. Under the circumstances he gave himself permission to open it, and he began reading with the last entry. When he finished, he looked over to the shelter. From what he'd just read, there was every reason to believe he'd find answers up there.

He was headed there when his phone vibrated. It was Suzen.

"I can hardly hear you. There's a lot of noise on the line."

"I'm outside, sorry." He moved behind a tree to get out of the wind. "Is this any better?"

"Alain, the oddest thing just happened. The guys here managed to get part of the system booted up. It was a monumental job, and it only stayed on for a few seconds before it shut down again. But it worked long enough to spit out some data that has me completely confused. I thought it might help you, though."

"How so?"

"It shows that about six o'clock in the evening Will got to the campground. I just checked your coordinates, and it's the same one where you are. According to his itinerary, he was supposed to overnight there, but it looks like he decided to keep going. I believe he was ahead of schedule, and we've seen him hike at night before."

"So you're telling me he left this campsite?"

"Yes and no. It's hard to tell what happened from this printout. It's what I'm hoping you can help figure out."

She explained the system had just spat out the report and she hadn't had time to analyze it. What was curious, though, was that it showed his gear scattered all over. A lot of it appeared to be near Harpers Ferry, and other things were still at the campsite. The report didn't show the exact location, only that it left. "If I didn't know better, I'd say it showed he split up with himself."

"Huh? It's difficult to hear you out here. Did you say, he split into pieces? What on earth do you mean?"

She spoke louder, and started from the beginning of the readout. She explained that an hour and a half after he arrived, the data showed some of his equipment left the area and went north.

"Wait. There's more. About a half hour after that — about nine-thirty — some of his other things left the site, again going north. So that explains why I'm seeing his stuff in Harpers Ferry. But, why? He should have been heading south. And here's something else that left very recently. About thirty minutes or so ago."

That would have been about ten minutes before Alain arrived, and he was eager to know if she could tell what direction the last bit went. Unfortunately, the output had degraded to the point of gibberish and no longer made sense. Unlike the other items that left, though, this one didn't appear to go back to the trail. According to the coordinates, it went into the woods.

"See how this is confusing?" She suggested that maybe he gave some of his things away, a T-shirt or two, maybe. "We both know he can be very generous."

Alain wasn't convinced. "Yes, but he knew the importance of not separating himself from his trackable gear." He asked her to break down the different tracks according to what piece of equipment went in which direction at what time.

"Sure, it might take a few minutes, but I think everything I need to give you is right here. Oh, and another thing. You know how it automatically calculates his speed? It looks like the first time stuff left, he was running. How could he run with all his gear?"

"I'm not sure it was him running."

When he asked if she could be more precise about the articles still at the campsite, she identified one item near him, and something else about fifty yards away. He looked around and noticed the tent. Then he walked back over to the shelter and crept up the steps. The body he found lying on the sleeping platform was covered by a dirty tarpaulin, but he could tell the person was tall enough to be his nephew.

"François!" he whispered, hoping it was loud enough to wake him. When there was no response, he removed his night goggles and walked closer. He gave the body a gentle poke. Nothing. Fearing the worst, he gently pulled back the tarp to reveal the man's head wearing François' stocking cap. What he saw next he'd seen before. A neck twisted around into an impossible and unnatural position. The head faced away, but he was grateful the cap was pulled all the way down over its face.

He simply couldn't bring himself to peek under the cap. Instead, he pulled back the tarp a little more. What it revealed knocked his breath away. Two large bloody fangs protruding from a menacing rattlesnake's head in an elaborate tattoo on the center of his bare chest.

It was all the confirmation he needed.

He quietly emptied the pockets and respectfully recovered the body again. Worried that emotions might cloud his judgment if he stayed a minute longer, he grabbed the little daypack and left the shelter. He'd go through the contents later, and his team would know how to handle the body properly.

He told Suzen about the tent, but he decided to tell her about the body later. They would have to keep a lid on the whole affair until he decided what information got released…and when.

Besides, his work up there was just getting started. He asked Suzen to remind him which way the last piece of gear went.

"Alain, I'm worried. Do you think he's all right?" Even with all the noise on the connection, she could hear the lump in his throat.

"I'm not sure how to answer that, Suzen, but from here, it looks like someone got to him before I did."

PART TWO

11

"Ask Me to Show You How to Poop in the Woods."

The letters were big and bold and written by hand on colorful poster paper. It was the first thing he saw on entering the Hiker Lounge. *A little late for that*, he thought. He'd been on the trail over a week already, failing at every aspect of hiking and camping. Now they're telling him he was probably doing that wrong, too. Too bad.

There had only been two people in the lounge for most of the afternoon, the guy on the couch and the guy at the terminal. When the newcomer entered the room they both looked up to give him the once-over. He was hard not to notice. Late-twenties or early thirties, tall and wiry with piercing deep blue eyes. Above them like a third eye was strapped his headlamp. He wore no hat, and his thick black hair was tamed and pulled back into one of those man buns. Most eye-catching, though, was his gear. The green backpack slung over one shoulder stood out against his black jacket. Both were high-end.

He wasn't the first hiker to show up with high quality gear, just one of the few. To be able to set aside a substantial enough amount of time to hike the whole trail, hikers generally fell into two groups: students and temporary dropouts from society. They were folks of all ages, who had tired of the daily grind and sought a morecarefree lifestyle. A life without responsibilities and many possessions. Because so many hadn't worked in months and ordinarily didn't have a lot of spending money, someone with expensive gear like this attracted attention.

He made a beeline for the free coffee from the large thermos in the corner. To get there he had to pass a hiker pecking away at the computer terminal along one wall. Maybe when the guy finished and the computer became available, he'd login, too. Try to find out if it was safe yet to leave the trail and go back home. He downed the first cup mechanically and stood there in a trance. Almost everything about the coffee was repugnant. It was thin and flavorless. To him, though, it was sustenance.

He poured a refill and gazed around the room when another sign on a wall caught his eye. Swap Box. One of the few people he allowed himself to speak with on the trail told him about it, and if it hadn't been for the sign he might have missed it. Turned out it comprised of not a box, but a teetering rack of plastic stackable bins. The guy said it was basically a bunch of free stuff. Free was his favorite price. What he hoped to find were fresh batteries for his headlamp, or better yet a whole new headlamp. It was tricky hiking the trail at night without one, and he didn't realize how fast his batteries would run down. He should have listened to the salesman in the store and bought some extras. Right now, he'd settle for a flashlight. In the city, he was a pretty tough guy, but the woods at night gave him the creeps.

"Pretty-slim pickings today, unless you wear a size seven shoe," boomed a voice from the other side of the room.

The newcomer turned his head in the direction of the voice and saw a clean-shaven guy slouched deep into the well-worn sofa. With his feet propped up on the rustic wooden coffee table, he looked as though he'd made himself at home. His attention went back to the Swap Box. Sure enough, the voice was right. Three pairs of worn smaller sized sneakers spilled out of the bins. He wore a size fourteen. At first glance there didn't appear to be much more. Under the sneakers, though, he spotted an opened package of water purification tablets. There were ten or twelve left. *Katadyn Micropur —effective against viruses, bacteria, cryptosporidium and Giardia.* Never in a million years did he think he would need to protect against anything as disgusting as whatever those things were. But he did now. He kept digging and turned up several partial rolls of toilet paper and a cheap plaid scarf. Still no batteries or even a flashlight, but not a bad find, considering he might have to go back out on the trail for at least another week or so. *Ugh*. He hated the thought.

The idea behind the Swap Box was all in the name. When you took something out, you put something back in. Southbound hikers would often leave heavy woolen caps and gloves for folks heading north. Everything had weight or took up space, even mittens, and they'd trade them in for lighter clothing. There wasn't much of value to him today, except the toilet paper. Everyone needed that, even those who hadn't been properly shown how to poop in the woods.

"Yeah, not much here," responded the new guy, still rummaging through the box. He spoke with one of those distinctive New York accents.

"It's the first thing everybody does when they come here. You never know what you're going to find," returned the voice from across the room. "And you know, most people need to dump stuff."

Not me, thought the newcomer.

The room grew silent, except for the clicking of the keyboard. The guy at the terminal had already turned back around and resumed his typing. The clicking pattern was typical of hikers messaging friends. A bunch of fast typing followed by a swat of the "Enter" key. Then a pause to read the response. Then another flurry of typing. Another swat. On and on.

Next to the computer terminal sat a real land-line telephone and above it a sign with a stern admonition, *Call Your Mother.* Some organization or another sponsored the phone, so hikers could call their mothers long distance free of charge. It seemed a bit of a relic, as almost everyone had cell phones, even hikers. They didn't use them often, though, because signals up on the trail were often missing or spotty at best. And even with the clearest reception, they had the challenge of keeping the batteries charged. Under the circumstances, Wi-Fi and a charging station might have been more practical feature to offer. Perhaps one day another flush group would sponsor one of those.

The hiker on the couch broke the silence again. He'd just finished reading a dog-eared copy of *The Dead of Winter,* a book he'd pulled from the lounge's other swap system. Next to the Swap Box sat a donated wooden bookshelf crammed with used paperbacks. Hardbound books took up space and were dead weight in a hiker's pack. While most of the books were about hiking, ecology and botany, there was one shelf of fun fiction.

"I just finished it," he said holding it up for the newcomer to see. "You like horror? It's supposedly set around here somewhere. Want to read it?"

"Yeah, maybe," he mumbled almost inaudibly. Guzzling the rest of his weak coffee, he returned to the coffee station to fill his cup a third time. Ignoring the guy at the other end of the room, he plopped down on a threadbare armchair and picked up the album of photos lying open on the adjacent table.

Most hikers passing through the Lounge at the Visitor Center had their picture taken, and each Polaroid was added to the vast collective of hikers through the ages. There were more binders full of hikers, all sorted chronologically, lining the bookshelf next to his chair. A color scheme explained by a chart on the wall identified the hikers by the direction they were hiking. A green dot on your photo meant you were headed southbound, and red meant northbound.

He appeared to be killing time as he flipped through the pages, until he focused on the last page and leaned in for a closer look at the entry dates. He assumed that like the rest of the stuff in the Hiker Lounge it was dated, but the most recent entries were made only a few days earlier. He didn't know Polaroid cameras still existed, and wondered where people got the film. Returning the album to the table he stared into space. He was sitting for about five minutes, when a loud rumbling sound came from inside his black jacket. It was louder than the only other sound in the room, the staccato cadences of the computer keyboard. After a short silence, his stomach let out another long growl.

"Sounds like somebody's hungry," joked the clean-shaven hiker from across the room. He was now reading a magazine.

Without turning to engage with him, the newcomer explained that he hadn't eaten in days. The hiker across the room laughed a little and said he was hungry too; it just wasn't as obvious. He pulled his feet off the table, stood up and walked over to extend a firm handshake. He was still in his stocking feet and wore one of those baseball caps with a fake black ponytail out the back.

"Hey, friend, I don't know your name. They call me Tracker." His wide smile revealed a mouth full of crooked teeth. One of his top front teeth gleamed silver.

Crap, the man thought. Why wouldn't the guy leave him alone? Now he was going to have to talk to him.

"Uh, Bill. Um, I'm Bill."

"Whaddya mean, Bill? You have another name, and I know who you are! You are...you're...let me think." After a dramatic pause he announced, "You're Growler. Get it? Yeah, Growler, that's going to be your trail name."

"Growler. Yeah, okay, fine." He shrugged and turned around.

Tracker looked up at the large clock on the wall. "Hey, Growler, it's almost six. You wanna grab some dinner?"

Growler said no to the invitation and explained he was a little short of cash. Tracker said he wasn't buying it. He knew Growler's jacket would have cost several hundred dollars. The backpack was expensive, too.

"You wouldn't expect to see a person with gear like yours to be broke. It's top of the line." Then he laughed again. "Maybe that's why you're out of money."

Growler explained he traded somebody for the stuff a while back, and he really hadn't paid much attention.

"I don't know what the other guy got out of the deal, but you definitely scored some nice gear."

Growler said the reason he was broke was because some guy stole all his money one night on the trail while he slept.

Tracker noticed he was wearing loafers and laughed again, asking if the same people stole his boots, too, adding if he planned to hike north he'd probably need to pick up a pair soon.

Growler, irritated at the man's persistence, said, "I'm fine, and anyway I'm heading south."

"Well, Growler this is your lucky day, because I happen to be loaded right now, and tonight your dinner is gonna be on me."

Growler made a weak effort at turning down the offer, but Tracker insisted. He said a guy who owed him money finally wired him some earlier in the day. It wasn't much, but he felt flush. Besides, he said he could use the company, and Growler was noticeably starving, so it was a win-win. He told Growler just to accept his offer and not be an idiot.

Growler followed with the obligatory empty promise to pay Tracker back one day, and they agreed to leave as soon as Tracker found his boots. He said he knew of a joint just up the street that was supposed to have pretty good food.

With one final smack with the index finger on the keyboard, the person at the computer pushed back from the desk and stood up.

"Oh, I forgot my manners. Lana Lang, meet Growler. Growler, this is Lana Lang."

Lana Lang? From the back, the oversize sweater and stocking cap gave Growler the impression the computer person was a guy, but now that the guy stood there facing him, there was no question about it. He, was a very attractive she. Growler looked over at Tracker, who returned his gaze with a little wink.

"Lana Lang? You mean like in Superman?"

"Superboy," she corrected. Her response was clipped, and she ignored his awkward attempt at a handshake.

From across the room Tracker asked if she had decided to take him up on the offer to go to dinner with him.

"If you're still buying," she said on her way to use the restroom. She made a point of adding she was only going because her boyfriend hadn't shown up yet.

As soon as she was out of sight, Tracker gave a fist pump. He confessed to Growler that she'd been putting him off all afternoon, and this was a real win. "Besides, I don't believe there is a boyfriend. I think she's just playing a game with me."

Growler couldn't have cared less, but he managed to wink back in male solidarity. While Tracker finished lacing up his boots, Growler wandered back over to the Swap Box. He wanted to make sure to take the toilet paper and the scarf before someone else got them. He didn't want Tracker to see him take the stuff out of the box, though, because he wasn't planning to put anything of his own back in. So, with his back to the room he attempted a little sleight of hand. While his left hand pretended to select a book from the shelf next to the Swap Box, his right hand easily slipped the toilet paper and other goodies into his pack. He wrapped the scarf around his neck, as though he'd worn it in.

"Hey, you still want to read this book, Growler?"

"Oh, yeah, I forgot." Tracker's question startled him, and he dropped the box of water purification tablets. They spilled out on the wooden floor, and he scrambled to pick them all up. He wondered if Tracker had been watching him the whole time.

"You won't regret it. It's the best one on the rack today. It's a fast read and it's really, really scary."

As he looked up from the Swap Box, Growler noticed another huge poster staring at him on the wall in front of him.

Bears Want Your Food! "Now that's what I call really, really, scary," he muttered.

The Hiker Lounge occupied a large back room on the first floor of the little gray stone Appalachian Trail Conservancy Visitor Center. The Appalachian Trail extended a little over two thousand miles from Maine to Georgia, and because of Harpers Ferry's location at about the midway point, the Visitor Center was a welcome and regular hangout for hikers going in both directions. It was a place to leave messages for other hikers and check up on one another, and it was conveniently located on Washington Street, the town's main drag. More and more hikers from nearby metropolitan Washington, DC, used Harpers Ferry as the entry point to the Trail, because from there they could hike smaller sections of it going north or south. The Visitor Center was the go-to place for everything non-hikers needed to know about the trail as well. Tourists stopped there, too, and there were plenty of them, because Harpers Ferry was an historic attraction, thanks in part to John Brown, his famous raid on the arsenal, and the poem that immortalized it by Stephen Vincent Binét.

The Gold Standard for hikers was membership in the Two Thousand Mile Club. You got that by hiking the entire trail within a year. "A year means three hundred and sixty-five days, not a calendar year," each volunteer at the Visitor Center never forgot to specify in their spiel. Perhaps they thought adding that detail made the four-to six-month task sound more doable.

Since most people couldn't devote such a large chunk of time all at once, volunteers enjoyed suggesting the many other options. Alternative thru hikes could be done as *flip-flops, leap frogs* and *wrap-arounds*, and they never tired of explaining the distinctions and how they worked.

As Tracker, Growler and Lana Lang left the lounge to make their way to the front door, they were stopped by a cheerful volunteer. She asked if they'd like her to take their photos. "Everyone wants to be in the book, you know, for posterity," she added with a touch of salesmanship.

Tracker shook his head, saying his photo already sat in a binder. She seemed pleased to hear that and asked Lana Lang and Growler if they were interested. Growler grunted a negative and held his hand over his stomach to indicate he felt too hungry. Lana Lang ignored her question entirely and elbowed her way out of the lounge ahead of the others.

For a late afternoon, the Visitor Center was quite crowded. People oblivious to closing time clogged the aisles between brochure racks and display counters of trail memorabilia. Souvenirs screamed *"I Did a Flip-Flop on the Appalachian Trail"* and *"I Can't Believe I Hiked the Whole Thing!"* Several tourists clutched fistfuls of free pamphlets, and two or three were engaged in spirited conversations with docents. A young man and woman in hiking clothes were studying a map of campsites and shelters.

It was a narrow fit to get to the front door. They had to squeeze between the couple, a swivel rack of postcards and a rather disheveled older gentleman with jet black hair studying some black and white photographs mounted on the wall next to the door. The old man was so engrossed that when Tracker accidentally bumped into him, he jumped in surprise. The old man fell backward, colliding into Growler, who lost his balance and wheeled around.

"Hey, watch where you're going!" Considering the whole incident was Tracker's fault, Growler seemed a little quick to get angry. His outburst attracted the attention of the others in the room. The old man grabbed Lana Lang's wrist for support and righted himself. She pulled her arm away as fast as she could.

"Oh, I'm so sorry, I wasn't paying attention and didn't see you," said the older man.

Growler stopped short of apologizing. "Yeah, okay," he mumbled on his way out the door.

"Wow. Did you get a whiff of the old man?" asked Tracker. "No wonder he fell down. I'm surprised he could stand up at all."

12

"The map room computer wasn't the only thing to catch a virus." It was Suzen. She'd spent the whole night at the office and only managed to sleep a few hours before returning late in the afternoon. Her body didn't know whether it should be awake or asleep. Nevertheless, she wanted to share what she just learned. Dillon had caught something, too, a human stomach virus that pretty much knocked him out all week. Since he was going to be the only one working that week, it explained why no one picked up the phone when Alain called. And no one returned his voicemails.

"Who's this Dillon guy again?" asked Alain. "And remind me why he was the only one working that week?"

She guessed they hadn't met yet, but she explained he was their new office manager. "If you remember, the upgrade to the new servers in the main GeoFibre office downstairs was going to take several days. Also, that the following Monday was one of our federal holidays. Since I was going to be out of the country anyway, I thought it would be a nice employee bonus to close the Foundation for the whole week."

"So, everyone was going to be gone?" Alain asked.

"No, not everyone. As I said, Dillon was going to make an appearance every day."

"Okay, let's recap," said Alain. "Somehow our tracking system was compromised, and we can't find Will. At the same time our office was completely unstaffed for an entire week. And all that happened while you were out of the country."

"What do you think it all means?"

"If nobody was in the office to know the tracking system was down, I'd have to say someone went to elaborate means to make sure we couldn't know Will's location last week. Or, I suppose it could just be a huge coincidence." He made a mental note to have his team do a complete rundown on this Dillon character.

"But who would have done that?" she asked.

"That's something I'll have to find out. But listen, I'm running out to grab dinner. I'll call you when I get back."

13

The restaurant was a bit of a walk down Washington Street, but Growler didn't mind adding three extra-long blocks to his day to get a free meal. Besides, it was nothing compared to the interminable time he'd spent on the trail. To celebrate his good fortune, he decided he would eat as much as he could get away with, without looking too greedy. And without being recognized. He hoped he'd been gone long enough and hiked far enough away by now to be safe. Still he couldn't afford to be reckless.

Figuring out how to eat on The Appalachian Trail ended up being his biggest problem. He simply hadn't given any thought to it at all. For someone with a large appetite, though, it was a serious misjudgment. Confronted with this harsh reality, he was forced to exit the trail often during the day to search for groceries in nearby towns. Since being seen in public was risky, his strategy was to hike at night. During the day he needed to sleep, and foraging for food interrupted his sleep patterns and made him grouchy. So, as soon as he got stocked up, he'd get right back on the trail as fast as he could to find a place to crash.

Bumming food from other hikers was much easier and certainly more convenient. He remembered the first time. The guy was a real talker, and not just light chitchat, either. He wanted to talk philosophy. To share their motivations for taking the plunge and hiking the trail. Growler told the guy that for him, it had all been 'rather spur of the moment' which was certainly sugar-coating it. His last job had gotten such publicity he needed to disappear, and fast. Vanishing into the woods seemed like an easy way, even though he started out unprepared in every way. Like wearing loafers and never having enough toilet paper, or food. Relaxing tonight on a real chair in a warm restaurant and ordering a free meal from an actual menu — now that was a real gift, and probably worth the risk.

From a block away, the aroma of sizzling steak told him they were close to something delicious, and he hoped it came from the restaurant Tracker picked.

Although just after six o'clock and country folks generally ate early, the restaurant was nearly empty. The middle-aged hostess with very bleached blonde hair sized up the group in no time at all. Two smelly guys and a woman, all with backpacks.

"Welcome to the White Horse. My name is Lucky. Y'all been hiking the Trail?" she asked, not really needing a response. They nodded back tentatively, hoping their hiker status wouldn't disqualify them from getting a table. Unfazed, she directed them to a tiny coatroom off to the left, where she said the management would prefer they leave their backpacks and other gear. She insisted their things would be safe.

Then she led them into the larger and darker back room to a long Early American style table in the corner. She referred to it as their Hiker Table, explaining that most hikers came to the restaurant in ones and twos, so they put them all together at one table. She hoped that would be all right. Growler made a production of hustling in fast and grabbing a spot at the far end of the table.

Tracker teased that maybe he picked the dark corner because he didn't want to be seen. "Let me guess. You're hiding from a woman, right? Ha-ha."

Growler pretended to laugh along with the joke, but he had to; Tracker was buying. Before he sat down, Tracker introduced himself to a couple who were already seated. The man looked to be about the same age, early thirties, and he sported multiple piercings in both lips and eyebrows. A huge, thick nose ring dangled behind two smaller ones, and two more delicate rings poked through the sides of his nostrils. His long droopy ear lobes sagged under the weight of shiny steel plugs an inch or so in diameter.

"Hardware," he said, with a knowing smile. It was his brand-new trail name, and he felt a little self-conscious saying it the first time. With his heavy accent, he struggled hard to pronounce the 'w.' "And dis is Moonbeam."

Moonbeam noticed Lana Lang staring at Hardware's ears. "Oh, these?" she asked, yanking playfully on his earlobes. "They're surgical steel tunnel gauges. He says everyone in Berlin has them."

Lana Lang's face conveyed her nonchalance. "They look like napkin rings," she said.

"Aren't German guys dreamy? We just met, and right away he said he'd hike with me. I'd say this little gal from Poughkeepsie did pretty well." Her voluminous hair was wild and multicolored, and she patted it constantly. When Lana Lang shifted her stare to her hair from Hardware's face, it was misinterpreted as engagement. "Um, yes, my hair is hand-painted, if that's what you were wondering. Some people say it's my best feature...though it's not my newest, if you know what I mean." She searched Lana Lang's face for compliments that never came.

The awkward exchange ended when Lucky came back with a stack of plastic menus, which she placed in the center of the table. Growler was the first to grab one, and when she saw him reach across the table, she gulped.

"Wow, those are the biggest hands I've ever seen!"

He did have huge hands, and it wasn't the first time he'd heard that comment, either. He learned long ago his hands weren't something he could easily hide, so ignoring her comment, he passed the menus to the others. He wouldn't need to consult one anyway. As long as the portions were big, he really didn't care what he ate. Since Tracker was paying for his dinner, though, he wasn't sure how it would work. Could he really order anything he wanted? It had been three whole days since he managed to bum food off another camper. And then there were those leftovers he scavenged at a campfire two nights earlier.

Tonight, though, was his lucky night. Even their waitress was named Lucky. If that wasn't a sign, he didn't know what was, and he hoped his luck would continue. If his current scrape with the law followed his regular pattern, another week or so in hiding was probably all he'd need before the authorities gave up and stopped looking for him.

In the meantime, he hated talking with strangers, and tonight his benefactor would probably expect him to make the effort to carry on a conversation in return for the free dinner. It was the least he could do. Tracker seemed harmless enough, and who knows, he might even be useful again. Besides, it appeared that Lana Lang was going to get most of Tracker's attention anyway, so maybe he'd be off the hook, after all. He didn't really care either way. After those dreary weeks on the trail he deserved a relaxing and fun night.

"Can I start you guys off with something from the bar?" Lucky's long hair was whipped around her head like soft serve ice cream, and when she raised up her hands to write the order on her pad, she exposed a long sentence scrolling around and up her left forearm. The swirl of the text matched her hairstyle, and the tattoo looked like a proverb or something in one of those popular and unreadable ancient Gothic or Celtic fonts.

Tracker was in a festive and generous mood. "What'll you guys have? Is everybody down with beer?"

Any fears Growler may have had about ordering too much were officially put to rest when Tracker said he would order for all three of them. And he made it simple. He wanted the biggest steaks in the house, with baked potatoes and sides of this and that. Growler was ecstatic.

"Lucky, these are my guests, so make sure they have whatever they want." He ordered the black bean burger for himself.

"You're a vegetarian, too?" asked Moonbeam, sensing a compatriot.

Tracker pointed to his crooked teeth, and bared his lips to show them off in a nonverbal explanation of his diet preferences. "Why, are you?"

"Oh, yes," she said a little smugly. "Eating animal flesh is, um, incompatible, um, with being spiritual." She shared a smile with Hardware. "We have so much in common. We're both, um, animal lovers."

When she spoke, her voice rose and fell in a studied cadence. Frequently, she would pause between phrases and emit a kind of humming sound before continuing, and the affectation seemed calculated to make her appear more spiritual and thoughtful.

When Lucky arrived with their drinks a few minutes later, she brought another diner to sit at their table, the older man from the Visitor Center.

"Like I said, the peach rosé is my personal favorite," Lucky bragged to her new customer, with a flirtatious twinkle in her eye. "But the rest of our wines are listed on the back of the menu."

The old man was grinning ear to ear and reeked of alcohol, and he let out a loud hiccup as he adjusted himself unsteadily into one of the available chairs. "I like to have a little glass of wine around the holidays," he explained with a comic touch.

"Sir, didn't we just see you down the street at the Visitor Center?" asked Tracker.

"Oh, I don't think so," he said studying each person at the table. He let out another hiccup and started to apologize for it, when a follow up hiccup cut his apology short. Then he steadied himself and broke into another big smile. "Say, now I do remember. You're the ones I bumped into."

"It's possible I knocked into you first," said Tracker. "Please accept my apologies, sir." He asked the old man to slide down and join them, and he made introductions to everyone at the table. There were muffled snickers as people moved their chairs to make room.

"Lana Lang, like in Superman, right?" he asked, and she repeated her predictable correction. "And you, young man, Tracker. It's nice to formally meet the man I knocked over."

"But we haven't really met formally, sir. You haven't told us your name yet."

The old man seemed surprised. "So I haven't. Hill," he said, extending his hand. "The name is Hill."

"I love your name It's such a perfect trail name," said Moonbeam.

"And, I adore yours. Say, haven't we met before?"

"Oh, no. That would be very, umm, unlikely. I've come from, umm, you know, *corporate*.

"Oh, well then, I guess we certainly couldn't have, could we? My mistake."

Growler was ready for more beer, and he flagged down Lucky. Mr. Hill put in his order by first declining the recommended peach rosé and opting instead for a glass of Burgundy. She noticed Lana Lang had hardly touched her beer.

"Anything wrong with your beer, Sweetie?"

Lana Lang cringed at Lucky's familiarity, and complained about it being too cold. Mr. Hill leaned in very close to her, and with a twinkle in his eye confided, "I don't like cold beer, either. And what do you want to bet that my Burgundy will come straight out of the refrigerator?"

Recoiling from his boozy breath, she slid to a seat farther away from him. While Mr. Hill studied the menu, Lucky arrived with two more hikers. The young men appeared to be in their late twenties and introduced themselves as Gear Guy and Streamin. Tracker assumed the role of host and made the introductions to the rest of the table. When he got around to presenting Hardware, Streamin's expression indicated they'd met before.

"Oh, yeah. Hi, again. We saw each other on the trail the other night, but I guess we didn't really talk. Nice to meet you."

"You know each other?" asked Lana Lang.

Hardware's face reddened. "Uh, no, not really. I guess I might have seen him once."

"And you, ma'am. It's nice to see you again, too," he said taking the empty chair next to Lana Lang.

"Huh? First, I've never seen you before," she grunted. "I've been stuck in this town for days. And second, I'm not a "Ma'am."'

Streamin shrugged it off and mumbled to the others that he was positive he saw her earlier on the trail. But he wanted to change the subject. "So, did you all have to come off the trail because of the bears, too?"

"Bears? What bears?" Moonbeam hadn't heard the news yet, but she admitted to being a little out of touch. "Since Hardware and I met, we've spent most of our time getting to know each other, if you know what I mean. We've hardly left our room," she giggled, staring into his eyes.

"Well, some official approached Gear Guy and me and told us there were reports of aggressive bears in the area. He encouraged us to visit Harpers Ferry for a few days, but we got the feeling it was more than just a suggestion, because he told us a few horror stories about some recent encounters. I think he was trying to scare us into coming to Harpers Ferry, but he didn't have to. He had us at *bears*."

"Hey, Growler! Remember that poster in the Hiker Lounge about bears wanting people's food? Maybe they should change it to, *Bears Want MORE than Just Your Food!*"

Everyone was still laughing at Tracker's joke, when Lucky returned with Mr. Hill's glass of chilled red wine. He gave Lana Lang a private little smile, as he cupped the glass with both hands. "Gear Guy, what an interesting name. Are you a mechanic?" He punctuated his question with another hiccup.

"Nah. I've just always been fascinated with gear — hiking equipment, tents, backpacks, all of it. I'm like the guy who knows everything about cars, but instead of transmissions, I get off on three-layer laminated fabrics and micro-seam allowances."

Streamin verified he'd seen Gear Guy in action. "He's a regular walking encyclopedia. Last night he went from person to person around the campfire, identifying what everyone had on, and a rundown of all the features."

Lana Lang was unimpressed. "Big deal. Half the time the name's right on the front."

"To tell the truth, Mr. Hill, your shirt has me a little stumped. But I'm really not that up on vintage stuff."

"So that's what my clothes are, vintage, huh?"

"I hope you don't think I meant any disrespect."

"Oh, none taken, (hic)."

"Mind if I take a look?"

"Go ahead. I think it's Bernbaum, or something like that." He pulled the top of his shirt around so Gear Guy could read the inside label.

"Hmm. Close. It's Berhnold, made in Switzerland. No wonder I didn't recognize it."

"So, did you buy it there?" Tracker shared winks and stifled giggles with the others.

"Oh, yeah, sure," said Mr. Hill, sharing in the joke. (hic). "No, but I think you can still get them at Nordstrom."

Tracker wanted to test Gear Guy's knowledge. The brand of his shirt wasn't on the front, but it didn't matter. Gear Guy easily pegged it as a house brand of a big box store.

"And a stinky one at that," interrupted Lucky. She pinched her nose with the fingers of her free hand as she set down the extra beers, and Tracker lifted his arms up to take a whiff.

"Seriously, is it that bad?"

Moonbeam made her humming sound again and commented that since becoming a vegetarian, she no longer needed to use deodorant.

"Then what's that smell?" groused Lana Lang, pretending to wave away the odor. "It's like church, or something."

Moonbeam thanked her for the perceived compliment and informed the table it was probably the Patchouli. She admitted to being a bit of an expert on essential oils. She sold them, too, and said she would be more than happy to set any of them up as distributors.

Lana Lang wanted no part in the game, and was quick to sideline Gear Guy's next demonstration. "Don't even start with me," she snapped. "I like to wear my boyfriend's clothes. So what?"

Tracker made a show of being devastated. "Oh, no! Not him again. You're breaking my heart." Then he made an aside to Gear Guy. Hey, at least we know he has good taste."

"You know who has great stuff? Growler. "His Arc'teryx Beta AR is the best, but man are they expensive. It's gonna be my next jacket, when I save up enough money." He guessed the green backpack in the coat room was Growler's, too. It was the Arc'teryx Altra 85 with Composite Construction Suspension. "I've never run across one in absinthe green outside of a store before."

"Yeah, I saw the same one a few days ago, too," said Streamin. "Not the exact same one of course, but another guy was wearing one just like it. The cool green that attracted my attention. Come to think of it, he had a black jacket like Growler's, too."

Gear Guy said he couldn't believe Streamin picked up on it, because he was always listening to music and never seemed to pay attention to anything. "It's lucky I didn't fall off a cliff. Streamin would never have noticed."

"Hey, that's not fair! Sometimes it's books on tape." Everyone got a good laugh, and nobody bothered to ask how he got his trail name. "But you know, the guy who wore Growler's stuff was very cool. His name was Red Rover, and he had top of the line everything, not just the pack and the jacket."

"Which way was he headed?" asked Tracker. "Maybe I'll run into him."

"You might, but I doubt it," said Streamin. "I have a feeling he's long gone by now."

14

"So, just how broke are you, Growler?"

Tracker's question was loud enough for everyone at the table to hear, and it was so personal it took Growler by surprise. He was afraid Tracker was going to renege on paying for dinner, and he had to think fast.

"Very broke. I told you, some creep stole my money on the trail a while back."

"First bears, now robbers!" Moonbeam clutched her throat and wanted to know what he was doing when they robbed him, and what the robber looked like. "Details. I want details." But she changed her tune when Growler explained his money was stolen while he was taking a dump in the woods. "Never mind. TMI."

"I only set the backpack down on the path for a few minutes while I walked into the woods. And it was in the middle of the day."

"Hold on. I thought you said someone stole it while you were sleeping? Anyway, it doesn't matter."

Tracker explained that he'd heard about a farm around Harpers Ferry that paid hikers cash for odd jobs. You camped out right on their property, and sometimes they even provided meals. Apparently, the owner of the outfitter shop and his wife sent hikers there all the time.

"Sounds like an easy way to make some quick cash, so I'm going. I thought you might like to come along, too. After I pay for dinner tonight, I'll be broke again."

Gear Guy and Streamin said they always needed money, and they suggested everyone hitch a ride together in the morning. Growler was an emphatic no. "There has to be an easier way to score some cash than doing manual labor for crap wages on some hick farm."

"What about you, Lana Lang? Want to join us for a couple days while you're waiting for your boyfriend?" He put boyfriend in air quotes.

"What's that supposed to mean? I wouldn't be caught dead working at some stupid farm! Besides, my boyfriend is probably already around here somewhere looking for me."

Moonbeam and Hardware also declined to work at the farm. Hardware was eager to start hiking, and they were going to take their chances on the trail first thing in the morning. "My guy's carrying a gun, and he promised to protect me from bears and robbers, so I'm not worried. Naturally, we're eager to make it an early night," she added with a wink. She took his hand and raised their arms as a testament to their bond.

Gear Guy pointed at Hardware. "Oh, my god. You just made me jealous!" Everyone looked a little confused except Moonbeam, who assumed Gear Guy found her attractive. "No, no. I meant Hardware's watch. He's wearing an Epix. Man, that's another thing I can't wait to get."

"Red Rover was wearing an Epix just like it," said Streamin. "They're way out of my league. I looked online. The basic model starts around seven hundred bucks."

"Hey, Hardware. Can you show me what you all are talking about?" asked Tracker. But Hardware pulled his sleeve down over it and ignored Tracker's request, and when Lucky suddenly arrived at the table with a solemn expression, Tracker's request was forgotten.

"Hey, what's the matter, Lucky? You look like somebody just died."

She looked over her shoulder and made a quick survey of the room. Once she was convinced nobody was looking, she slid onto an empty chair and said she had something serious to tell them. As an extra precaution, she made a fan with her menus, ostensibly to block the view from the only other couple in the room.

"Look, I don't want everybody and their brother getting nervous, so this is for your ears only. Darryl back in the kitchen just heard some terrible news he thought you should know about." She put her hand to her chest and swallowed. "He's got a police scanner and it's been going crazy with chatter about a body they just found on the trail. A dead body."

"A dead body? Where?" blurted Moonbeam, forgetting to add one of her 'umms.'

Lucky shushed her right away and reminded them about not starting a panic. It would no doubt be in the papers soon enough. In deference to Lucky, whispered questions came rapid fire from the group. Where did they find the body, and did they know who it was, and was it a hiker? She filled them in with a few details. The victim was a male with a beard, probably early thirties. Tall, and yes, a hiker. They found him covered with a tarp on the sleeping platform of a shelter a few days' hike from Harpers Ferry.

"I wonder if it's Shady Pines campsite," asked Streamin. "I was just there."

On her next trip to their table, Lucky confirmed that it was Shady Pines, and she had some additional information. "The guy had no identification and was apparently naked from the waist up. Why do you suppose that was?"

"Does this mean nobody knows who he is?" asked Lana Lang.

"One of us must have seen him," said Gear Guy. "We're all hiking the same direction, aren't we? South?"

Growler begged to differ. "Don't look at me. I've been going north."

"I could have sworn you said you were going south. Remember we talked about your loafers?"

Growler dismissed it with a snort. "Did I? I was probably so hungry I wasn't thinking straight. Oh, no. I'm definitely heading north."

"Red Rover, I wonder if it could be Red Rover?" asked Streamin. "He fits the description. You know, the guy with Growler's pack." Then he quickly apologized. "You know what I meant."

Growler was getting tired of their obsession with his backpack, but he brushed it off. Streamin continued.

"Last time I saw Red Rover, he was setting up camp at Shady Pines Campsite. I remember because we talked earlier about hiking straight into Harpers Ferry and hanging out together. He said he'd changed his mind and decided to hike straight on through. I didn't ask him why."

Tracker and Lana Lang insisted they'd never set eyes on this Red Rover person, and Moonbeam and Hardware pleaded ignorance, too, but Streamin looked puzzled.

"Hey, now I remember. Lana Lang, that's where I saw you. I passed you on the trail near Shady Pines, around the same time I saw Red Rover. It was late, and there were only a couple of people still hiking."

Lana Lang rolled her eyes. "I just told you I wasn't there. I've been stuck here in this dumb town waiting for my boyfriend."

Streamin persisted. He remembered she'd been with a guy. He hadn't seen her friend's face, but he recalled he spoke with an accent like Hardware.

"Was it him?"

She rolled her eyes again and once again said she had no idea what he was talking about.

"Are you sure? I mean, I'm positive. Don't you remember me, we...?"

Finally, she lost her patience. "How am I supposed to remember every stupid hiker who passes by?" She stood up. "Does anyone know where they keep the bathrooms around here?"

Streamin pointed to a sign he'd seen over by the bar, and she asked if he would show her. When they turned into the hallway and were out of sight, she grabbed him by the collar and yanked him to her face.

"Look," she whispered. "Let's get this clear. Of course, I remember you, but let's keep that between us, okay? My boyfriend is the jealous type, and he won't like hearing that I was hanging around with some other guy. And I don't want that bimbo at the table to know I was with her guy. Besides, nothing happened. It was a nice day, and we were just out for a little walk."

When she returned from the restroom she pretended to use, Lucky was back at their table. Her friend Ranger Cody had stopped by earlier with some fresh details. It seems they found a small daypack next to the body and a tent pitched just steps away from the shelter. They figured it belonged to the deceased. Gear Guy immediately wanted to know what kind of pack it was.

"Wouldn't knowing what was in the thing be more valuable than knowing the brand?" asked Lucky. She was puzzled by his question, but Gear Guy insisted a brand name would tell him a lot about the owner.

She had more information. When the authorities first got the call, they assumed it had been the result of one of those bear attacks that were happening more recently, but it only took the coroner a few minutes to rule that out. Now they were calling it a homicide. The victim had been dead for a couple days, and his neck was broken, by someone with strong hands. Nobody could resist glancing at Growler.

"Whoever did it must have known what they were doing, too, they said, because the victim was at least six feet. He only had a little cash on him, so they didn't think it was robbery. Still no name. At least, if the authorities know who it is, they aren't saying."

"Gosh, who would want to kill a hiker?" Tracker asked somberly.

"Another hiker, apparently. At least that's who they suspect. Oh, my gosh. It's not one of you, is it?"

Before she left Lucky gave them a little heads up. "Tomorrow is going to be wild around here. The place will be crawling with cops."

"The trail already is," said the tallest of three new hikers who had just appeared at the table. He introduced himself as Tornado and quickly recognized Growler. "Long time, no see."

"Huh? Oh, yeah," said Growler shifting uncomfortably in his chair. "What exactly do you mean by crawling with cops?"

Tornado corrected himself. Technically, they were rangers, not cops, and they had already sealed off several sections of the trail. It was bears again, and they weren't letting anyone enter the trail for about fifty miles in either direction, until the authorities made sure it was safe. Anybody already in that range had to exit the trail at Harpers Ferry.

"They gave us a ride all the way here."

"Great. Now I have to stick around even longer," groused Lana Lang.

"Like I said, it being a homicide an' all, they are going to want to talk to all of you." Lucky hadn't meant to eavesdrop, but she overheard them mention working at Ridgefield Orchard. "You know, it's not far from town, and if you left early enough in the morning, you could probably get out of here before the authorities showed up."

Growler was the first to change his mind. "Tonight's been a lot of fun. I'd like to hang out with you guys at the farm for a few more days. You know, until things cool down."

"Well, I'm going to the cops," announced Streamin. "I can't say I knew Red Rover, but I could at least identify the body, if he was the victim."

"Maybe there's a picture of him in the Hiker Lounge," offered Tracker. "Do you think you'd recognize him from a photo?"

"Of course, I'd recognize him anywhere." Streamin would see the cops first thing in the morning, if it was alright with everyone. Growler was the only one to grumble. He was really looking forward to farm life, and hoped Streamin wouldn't take too long.

"Mr. Hill, have you ever run into this Red Rover character?" asked Tracker. When Gear Guy pointed out that Mr. Hill had nodded off, Tracker elbowed the old man gently in the ribs. He abruptly sat up straight and pretended to be wide awake. Tracker repeated his question.

Mr. Hill admitted his powers of observation clearly weren't what they used to be and reminded them he hadn't even recognized Lana Lang, Growler and Tracker from earlier that evening. And that was after literally knocking them over.

"So, no, I don't think so. But the way you guys are talking about him, I hope I do. He sounds fascinating."

Lucky checked on the table and asked if Mr. Hill would like another glass of wine. He declined, and with a straight face told the group he maintained a strict one drink limit. That one-drink limit line was to become one of the standard jokes the rest of the evening, nearly always followed by a loud hiccup from someone in the group. Then he announced it was considerably past his bedtime, and he still had some important things to do.

He seemed wobbly when he stood up, but he made sure to make the rounds and shake hands with each of them. As they watched him stagger out of the room, Streamin said he was a little concerned, and said he'd follow him out.

"I'm concerned too," said Growler. "Concerned he might stiff us."

It didn't take long after Mr. Hill was safely out of earshot, for them to start poking fun at him. Moonbeam admitted she couldn't take her eyes off his cheap wig, and wondered if he really thought he was fooling anybody.

"I'm a hair person, you know. I notice these things."

Gear Guy came to Mr. Hill's defense. "Hey, what's with all the judgment? So what if he had a goofy wig and he liked his wine?"

"Don't look at me," said Tracker. "I don't judge. With teeth like mine I can hardly make fun of someone else's looks. Took a hockey stick in the mouth as a kid and always thought I'd get it fixed when I got the money. Then life happened."

"Talk about cheap — what about Growler's scarf?" asked Gear Guy.

Everyone took another look at the scarf he'd taken from the Swap Box and burst out laughing. They agreed it was about the ugliest thing any of them had ever seen.

Lucky brought them enough juicy tidbits to keep them drinking and talking for another hour, but when the pipeline of information finally dried up, Tracker asked for the check.

"I hope you kept them separate," said Gear Guy. "With all the beers everyone ordered, it'll be a nightmare to figure out who got what."

"Oh, believe me, honey, I did," she said, snapping her gum. "We're professionals around here."

Tracker wasn't worried. He explained to the rest of the group that he had offered to pay for himself, Lana Lang and Growler. The old man only had one glass of wine and some

French fries, so even if he did skip out, it wasn't going to break the bank, and he'd cover him too. Moonbeam dug around in her bag and produced a hundred-dollar bill, which she waved in the air and ceremoniously slapped down on the pile of cash the others contributed. It should more than cover her and Hardware, she slurred, knocking over a glass of water in the process.

"So, we're still meeting tomorrow at nine, right?" Tracker looked around to be sure everyone was on board with the plan. They were to meet up at The Beanery, a joint just up the street on the corner, and the only place open in the morning at that end of town. Gear Guy and Growler nodded yes.

Lucky appeared again with hot coffee, seven mugs and apple pie for everyone. "I hope you left room for dessert," she joked.

"Hey, we're not paying for that," insisted Growler, and Lucky shushed him right up.

"The dessert and coffee are courtesy of the older gentleman who left a while ago. He asked me to serve it at the end of the evening to make sure you all sobered up."

"That's a good one," said Tracker. "He wanted to sober us up."

"Oh, and he paid all your checks, too. Even left me a big tip."

15

The quality of the natural light was ideal to take the snapshot. In the late afternoon the combination of light and shadow was the most flattering. Sitting on a low brick wall in front of the stone building, the young man in the Polaroid struck a pose like a professional. One sneakered foot rested on the ground, and the other atop the wall, his right arm casually draped around his bent knee.

Though hardly a professional photographer, in that split-second the volunteer caught the hiker in a perfectly relaxed and carefree moment. He was playfully twirling around his wool stocking cap on the index finger of his left hand. Next to him on the wall sat his absinthe green backpack. A wide goofy smile teetered on the verge of a laugh, and his open mouth exposed perfectly straight white teeth. Even the lens of the cheap Polaroid camera loved him.

The sleeves of his sweater were pushed up and revealed something needing closer examination. They brought a magnifying glass, and he leaned in closer. The elaborate watch on the young man's tanned arm came into view.

A finger tapped lightly and repeatedly on the photograph at the top left corner of the page in the open binder and labeled with a green dot sticker.

"Yep, that's him, Red Rover."

"Are you sure?"

"It's absolutely him. And that's his watch and backpack."

Ranger Cody thanked him, adding that identifying the hiker was invaluable and would save them all a lot of time. And that more than likely, the other information might also prove to be helpful, too.

"It was really fortunate I happened to be here tonight. This place is usually closed this late."

The young man said he took a chance and saw the light on. He was glad to be of service, but he was in a hurry to get back to his friends.

16

"It never fails to surprise me what people say when they believe they are in the presence of fools and drunks, Suzen. Tonight's dinner conversation was most informative."

"At least now I know what you meant when you told me you were 'in the field.' You had a whole restaurant to set up."

It wasn't that difficult to make the White Horse look like it was open for business again. When it folded a few years earlier and the owners abandoned the building, they left all the fixtures and kitchen equipment behind. Major M provided the manpower to get it cleaned and Alain only needed a staff of one. Lucky did a good job talking most everyone into ordering the same thing, which made bringing it in from a nearby diner so easy. Moonbeam threw them a loop by ordering vegetarian, but Alain was pleased the way they pulled that off, too.

"I can just picture someone named Darryl back in the kitchen listening to the police scanner," laughed Suzen.

"I know. Lucky came up with that idea. It was brilliant. Having Darryl back there allowed her to keep the suspects together at the table longer by spreading out the news."

"His staff was already transcribing the dinner conversation Alain had secretly recorded, and they would be up late working up profiles of each hiker from both what they said and their reactions to others. While that was in the works, the FBI fingerprinting lab down the road in Martinsburg, West Virginia, would be analyzing the prints Lucky pulled from the glassware. Alain thought it was likely that at least one of them would have some sort of record. Maybe he'd at least get a couple names.

In his field, it was not uncommon to deal with an alias or two, but he had to laugh. Everyone in this pool of suspects had at least one. It was built into the DNA of the Appalachian Trail. And not just the suspects; he had one, too. Suzen was wary of his choice, because *hill* was one of the translations of the French *mont*, and she was concerned someone would make the connection.

"When was the last time you ran into an American with a working knowledge of French?" he asked, defending his pick.

Lacking the real identity of a suspect wasn't anything new for him. Le Mauvais was a perfect example. If the papers hadn't given him that name, no one would have known what to call him. For now, he'd be content with using their trail names.

Another coincidence added to his challenge. All the men were about the same age, size and build. Growler was slightly taller and darker, and he sported the man bun, but the rest had long hair, too. And hair color and style was the easiest thing to change. With this crop of suspects, Alain wasn't convinced the description he'd wanted at the outset would be of much help.

They did have a couple of data points to investigate. While Moonbeam was obviously her trail name, she did mention her previous employment at GeoFibre. And thanks to the peach rosé, she let slip she was from Poughkeepsie. Suzen hoped there wouldn't be too many female employees in the GeoFibre HR files from there, and she initiated a search right away. The company had grown significantly since the days when she knew each one by name, but off hand she didn't recall anyone as voluptuous as Alain's description.

"Oh, I doubt she looked anything like she does now. In fact, she bragged that her newest feature was her breasts. Tornado is as res-blooded as they come, and he said Moonbeam's boobs look fake. He guessed she probably had some other nips and tucks done as well."

Alain knew she wasn't a suspect. Still, there was more than just the GeoFibre connection that struck him as odd, and he wanted to know all he could about her. Growler, on the other hand, was the textbook definition of shady. Several times throughout the dinner he'd been caught telling lies. White lies, mostly, and Alain couldn't figure out why Growler bothered telling them, since they dealt with seemingly inconsequential things, like which direction he was heading, and how his money and food were allegedly stolen. His hands, too, looked capable of the signature executions. The fact that Growler was in possession of François' coat and absinthe green backpack was indisputable and for now, the most damning. Lucky had verified that with a quick trip to the coatroom while they were eating. Alain knew, though, that simply having the stolen goods didn't mean Growler killed for them. But it did make him the number one suspect.

"Our list is pretty short. Do you think it's possible the killer is still out there and we've just missed him somehow?"

"I don't see how. Our team sealed off the trail for fifty miles on either side of the shelter, and our drone coordinator reported we've covered every square centimeter of our target area. It's hard to imagine anyone sneaking past us. No, I firmly believe I've met him and just don't realize it yet.

Then he laughed and told her she might get enjoy hearing about the completely unexpected relationship triangle he discovered was a foot.

"You know, Suzen. I've got to admit, that when it was revealed that Hardware was not only having a relationship with Moonbeam, but that possibly with Lana Lang as well, I nearly lost it. I think it was the denials from the guilty parties that triggered my imagination, and I began to concoct elaborate schemes and cover ups. To prevent me from staring at them like a teenager I had to keep making those crazy hiccups."

"Good grief! Can you really think that all three are somehow connected in some way to your assassin?"

"Well, that's just it. I had to stop and remind myself that the simplest explanation is usually the right one."

"And what's that?"

"It's that Hardware is a serious lady's man, and that what we have going on here is a good old-fashioned *ménage à trois!*"

17

Why is this getting so complicated? It should have been so easy. Track him, kill him, and scram. I should've split as soon as it was done. Why did I have to stick around and make sure I got the right guy? I never miss. Now the cops are getting involved. I'll outsmart them, but still…something's starting to smell funny.

18

Despite the gift of coffee, not everyone would leave the restaurant sober. Early in the evening Moonbeam proclaimed that her first hike with her new guy called for something festive, and she decided upon the White Horse version of a Cosmopolitan. She found the cocktail so delicious, she followed the first by two more. For the remainder of the evening she babbled on about how they brought such clarity to her thoughts. That and later the whole bottle of peach rosé.

"Did I menshun I was in corporate? At GeoFibre. I even knew the owner." Then with an exaggerated wink to Tracker and Lana Lang, she slobbered, "I think he had kind of a thing for me."

"I'll bet he did," said Lana Lang.

Tracker needed to help her up from the table and walk her all the way through the restaurant and out the door, and when they got to the sidewalk, he gladly released her to the custody of a slightly less-inebriated Hardware. Leaning into each other for support, they staggered down the main street to the town's hostel. They understood the door would be unlocked. Hikers dropped in late at night all the time, and the owners learned long ago it was easier to let people find a bed by themselves and settle with them the next morning.

Growler had kept Lucky and the bartender busy all night, and he was toasted. Since he wasn't paying, he figured he'd keep drinking until Tracker cut him off, which he never did. Gear Guy, on the other hand, managed to nurse two beers the entire evening. He was sober and not ready to call it quits. Earlier that afternoon he checked into the Harpers Ferry campground, where he knew he could take a long hot shower. Since he'd already set up his tent it wouldn't matter how late he stayed out. The campground was just across the highway and only about a twenty-minute walk from town.

Tracker hadn't made any plans, but he had a great idea. Up the hill behind St. Peter's Catholic Church was the famous lookout, Jefferson Rock. He understood there were plenty of places where you could roll out sleeping bags. "Any takers?"

"Is it far?" asked Growler.

"Nah. You must have passed by it on your way here."

Growler knew exactly where it was, but the idea of sleeping near a famous landmark sounded risky. He'd been out in public for much longer than he wanted to be, and he was eager to crawl back into the shadows as soon as possible. Still, it was late, and the price was right. Besides, soon enough he'd be safe on a farm in the middle of nowhere. Then he remembered passing by a secluded spot up there near the rock formation. He could crash there.

"I'm in," he said.

"How about you, Lana Lang? Want to join us?" asked Tracker.

She didn't respond. He turned around to see she had stopped and was engaged in conversation with a woman locking up a small storefront office. The sign in the window said for just fifty dollars, a dog in a local shelter could be spared from being euthanized. It was the last day for people to step up, and the woman was shaking her head. People had been generous, she explained, but due to budget shortfalls there were still several that would have to be put to sleep. Tracker heard Lana Lang ask how many animals were at risk. Then he saw her hand the woman four one-hundred dollar bills.

"Bless you, bless you!" Lana Lang squirmed away from the woman who tried to give her a big hug in thanks.

"Wow, what a nice thing to do," said Tracker. Her generosity seemed so at odds with her caustic personality. "What made you do that?"

"I had a stray once," she replied, staring at the photos of the strays on the window.

Tracker sensed a chink in her armor and made a move. "So, what do you think, Lana Lang? Are you going to join us?"

"I can't think of anything worse." She abruptly turned right at the corner and never looked back.

The four guys continued down Washington Street, passing little tourist shops tucked into the stone confines of buildings dating to the late 1700s. Soon Washington Street became High Street, and after a few more blocks up the steep steps toward the church, the midway point to Jefferson Rock. The spire doubled as a cellphone tower, and the blinking light shone clearly at night.

Tracker could not help being impressed that as drunk as Growler was, he seemed to know where he was going and took the lead. "Hey, Growler?" he asked. "How do you know this place? Have you been here before?"

"How could I? I'm going north, remember."

"South, north, south, north. Are you just playing with us?"

It wouldn't ordinarily have been a very challenging climb for the young hikers, but after a night of heavy drinking Growler found himself needing to stop at every landing to catch his breath. He huffed and puffed and complained constantly.

Even without the benefit of moonlight, they saw the small wooden sign pointing to the bottom of the famous last flight of steps leading them to Jefferson Rock.

"Are you kidding me? Sixty-four more steps after this?" Growler was both wasted and tired. He'd had enough. Then he saw his spot, the ruins of St. John's Episcopal, a church that burned down and was abandoned over a century ago.

"Hey guys, I'm going to crash here," he said.

"No way, Growler! You've gotta at least come up to the top with us for a few minutes. If I can do it, you can," said Gear Guy.

Tracker called over, "You can always go back down to your ruins later."

Gear Guy began to count the steps out loud. "Someone said there are sixty-four. Let's see if they're right."

The steps were very steep in parts, but remarkably they got to the top in only a few minutes. They found rock to rest on while they took in the panorama. Even at night Jefferson Rock commanded a breathtaking view of the Shenandoah River.

Tracker asked Streamin if he wanted to change his mind. "If you spent the night, you could wake up with this view at sunrise."

"I have no intention of seeing the sun rise," laughed Streamin, and he reiterated his intention of staying in a warm bed at the hostel. In the meantime, though, he was a little sleepy from his full day of hiking, and he found a spot on one of the long flat boulders and said he would lie down for a minute. In no time he was asleep.

Gear Guy decided to stick around a little while longer, but he still planned to spend the night at the campground.

"Too bad Lana Lang isn't here," said Tracker. "I bet she would have enjoyed the view."

"I still don't get what you see in her," said Growler. "She's such a bitch."

Streamin's heavy snoring interrupted their conversation. Growler noticed and said, "That's another reason you don't want me up here with you. They say I snore."

"You're right. We wouldn't want you sleeping up here with us, but before you go, let me tell you about this place." Tracker stood up and assumed the role of tour guide. "Most people don't realize Jefferson Rock is located right on the trail and those of them going south have to pass by again. Look, even in the dark you can tell the Shenandoah River and the Potomac River converge down there. Technically, it's called a confluence of the two rivers. Did you know Jefferson bragged to Europeans it was worth crossing the Atlantic just to see it, and for all his public relations, in time the country named the formation for him."

"When did you become some kind of history expert?" Growler gave Tracker a poke to the middle of his chest. It was only meant to be a little horseplay, but he was drunk and overplayed both the joke and the poke. It caught Tracker off guard, the push enough to make him lose his balance. He lost his footing, too, and started to skid sideways down the smooth flat rock.

"Holy crap!" he cried, as he slipped farther down. Falling off the edge would mean certain death.

Growler reached out to grab Tracker's arm, but his timing was off, and he was short by a foot or so, and Tracker kept slipping, closer and closer to the precipice, seconds from going over the edge. Without thinking, Gear Guy flung himself into the air toward the vertical rock wall to the left of the precipice and Tracker. When his back slammed against the rock it stopped his fall. He hung onto a tree root with one hand, and reached out to Tracker with his other.

"Grab on!" he shouted. With only a couple inches to spare, Tracker caught his hand and Gear Guy pulled him to safety.

"You saved my life, Gear Guy."

"Yeah, well, what else would I do? Let you fall off and be the one to desecrate Jefferson Rock for all eternity? I think one dead body on the Appalachian Trail is enough for one day, don't you?"

"I didn't mean to push you so hard," insisted Growler. "I was just kidding around!"

They ignored him as they crawled on their hands and knees up the slippery rock and onto the safety of solid ground. Growler tried again to claim innocence, but when he finally figured out they were ignoring him, he stopped talking. After a minute or so, he announced he was going back down to the ruins. No one responded, but they heard the sound his loafers made as he went back down the steps.

Gear Guy and Tracker sat on the ground and stared into the darkness below.

Then Tracker broke the silence. "Someday, when I'm on my feet, I'll find a way to pay you back for this."

"That's okay, Tracker. You would have done the same for me." Then he joked, "Besides, you have a tooth to fix first."

Tracker was serious, and asked Gear Guy for his contact information. Gear Guy dug around in his pack and found a little card he brought along just in case.

"Yeah, look me up sometime if you feel like it. It would be fun."

Tracker glanced at the card and slipped it in his pocket. After all the excitement he felt a little tired, and said he was ready to crash.

"I don't blame you, but I think I'll stick around for a while to make sure you're okay, if you don't mind."

"Thanks, but I think I'll be all right, as long as I stay away from that rock."

"And Growler," Gear Guy added with a little laugh.

Tracker rolled out his sleeping bag. "I still can't believe that goofy Mr. Hill bought us all dinner, can you? Thanks to him, I didn't have to use much of my own money. It's right here, see?" He unzipped a pocket of his backpack, and Gear Guy saw the bundle of crisp bills.

"In case I go over another cliff, I want you to have it, okay?"

Gear Guy stared at the sky without responding. By now Tracker was lying flat on his back and drifting off, and Gear Guy let him.

Then Tracker surprised him by mumbling again. "Even though I don't need the money right now, I'm still gonna go work at that farm. You know, get off the trail for a while. What about...?" Then he nodded off without finishing his question.

"What about me?" Gear Guy stood up and slung his bag over his shoulder. "Yeah, I'm definitely going there, too."

19

Major M expedited the delivery, and had the device Alain found in the ashes at the campsite flown to the GeoFibre main lab in Montreux for immediate analysis. It was a good thing they had the extra time, too, because for a whole day the gadget mystified the experts. Given there were earbuds attached, it looked a bit like a crude version of an iPod, and considering the environment in which it was found – on a trail popular with young people – it made sense. Opening it revealed something quite different and much more complicated.

The pulsing light Alain told them caught his attention was the battery telling him it was just about dead, a small matter for the scientists to determine the proper voltage and power it up. An analysis of some of the components led one person to suggest it might act more like a Geiger counter. But they still were at a loss to figure out what it was intended to measure.

They considered the context in which it was found. What kind of equipment would a hiker be carrying? Could it be a metal detector? People were always searching beaches and other areas for artifacts. But this device didn't register metal, or anything else they put it near. It became even more unlikely that it belonged to a hiker when they discovered a type of sensor built into one end.

Now all they needed to determine was what it was supposed to sense. After that, it would be up to Alain de Beaumont to figure out why he found it discarded near a campfire.

20

"Can You Help Us Identify this Man?" The posters were taped to the front door, on the windows, and one was even slapped on the front of the cash register of The Beanery that morning. Somebody had done a lot of work on a Saturday night to get them printed and put up. But then, when there's a dead body found anywhere on the Appalachian Trail a lot of people can get involved — federal, state and local people.

The Appalachian Trail originally had its own rangers, but when officially designated a National Scenic Trail by Congress in 1968, things started to get complicated. With its new federal protection, the National Park Service and the USDA Forest Service also had jurisdiction. In some places the trail ran over non-federal government lands, making it more than a little confusing to know exactly what kind of infraction triggered which legal entity. In a case involving a dead body, determining which of these entities had jurisdiction depended on exactly where the body was found, and whether there was foul play. The Department of State would get involved if the deceased was a foreigner, and at the slightest suggestion of terrorism all the others would be trumped by the Department of Homeland Security. That morning, though, the onslaught of any authority had yet to arrive. For now, it was only the flyers, and they were the work of Ranger Cody.

To any of the locals, the three-sided shelter in the large photo would look familiar enough. One could find structures like this one up and down the trail like rest stops on a toll road. What wasn't ordinary about the photo was the body of the tall, shirtless, lifeless man stretched out on the shelter's sleeping platform. Ranger Cody redacted the face with a hastily made, but strategically placed big black dot. Next to the body sat a small daypack. The poster copy urged anyone who knew anything at all about the identity of this man to "contact the authorities immediately."

It was unclear, though, just which authorities.

Alain de Beaumont made a point of arriving early, and he sipped his coffee alone in a corner booth with his back to the room. Tracker had designated this the meeting place for everyone going to work at the farm. The plan had been for them to hitch a ride, and Alain was eager to see who would show up. It would tell him a lot.

Gear Guy arrived first, and he commandeered a table in the center of the room. For being the only place open at that hour, he was surprised there wasn't much of a crowd. The few couples scattered around were buzzing about the poster and the tragedy that happened only a few miles away. The woman suggested it was a drug overdose, because they had become so commonplace, and her husband blamed the lack of a military draft for creating a generation of ne'er-do-wells.

"From what I heard, they're saying it was a homicide," Becky told him as she poured his coffee. "The poor guy had his neck snapped, you know...execution style." She pantomimed the act with her hands and accompanied it with the glottal sound she thought described the action. *Gack!*

"Why in the world would anyone want to kill a hiker?" asked Gear Guy, wishing he had a newspaper.

Each time the door to The Beanery opened, a tiny little bell at the top tinkled before it slapped against the glass pane. This time, the tinkle was followed by a thud, made when the small bundle of newspapers hit the floor just inside the door. It was just loud enough to cause the young cashier to look up from her texting. With a shrug and a sigh of reluctance she set her phone down and shuffled across the room. Gear Guy beat her to it.

"Here, let me do that," he offered, stooping to pick up the bundle. The headline blared the revelation in giant type. "Oh, my god, people! You've got to see this!"

The not-very-noisy room became even quieter as he read the headline aloud to the other table.

Tech Billionaire Believed Missing on Appalachian Trail.

"Do you think he's the same person as the dead guy in the poster?" the woman asked.

"The article only says he's missing, not that he's dead," said Gear Guy. "Anyway, jeez, I hope not. I mean, this guy is one of my heroes."

"Who is he?" asked Alain from his corner booth.

"William François Chillon de Beaumont," Gear Guy answered confidently. "We all studied him in business school. He's a major tech superstar." He suggested some of them probably had heard about his invention, the Doodad. "You know, that thing that keeps track of your stuff." By now there were several knockoffs on the market, and you could buy them everywhere.

"I think my nephew has one hooked to his car keys," offered Alain, his back still to the room.

"Well, I'll be," said the woman. "You can get to be a billionaire by inventing something like that?"

Gear Guy summarized the rest of the article about how GeoFibre had been monitoring Will's location through the labels sewn in his clothes. Becky asked the same question that plagued them all. How in the world could the guy who invented something that finds lost objects end up being lost himself? It seemed inconceivable.

"I know. It doesn't make sense. There had to be some kind of glitch in the system," said Gear Guy.

He read in the article about an agreement William had with his company, that if for some reason they lost track of him for seven days in a row they were to call in the troops. Literally. "That means he has been missing for a whole week!" he lamented.

"It might just a bad signal up there," offered Becky. "We have a terrible one at our house, and we live right here in town."

The newspapers sold out quickly, everyone so engrossed in the story they finished their breakfasts in silence. Even Becky refilled their cups on tiptoe.

Gear Guy still looked confused. "The article doesn't explain how, with all their electronics, they could lose track of him."

"I bet someone's in big trouble!" came Alain's voice from the booth.

At exactly nine am the tiny bell tinkled again, and Lana Lang walked in. She sat down at Gear Guy's table, looking at the wall clock. "Where's everyone?" she barked. "I thought we were meeting at nine."

Gear Guy looked up over the top of his paper. "Don't ask me. And what are you doing here, anyway? Last night you told everyone you wouldn't be caught dead working on a farm."

She shrugged. "The longer I thought about it, the more I decided I'd be safer there. A single woman hiking alone can't be too careful, you know."

"But what about your boyfriend?"

"Who? Oh, him." She stumbled a little with her response. "He'll just have to wait around for a couple of days, won't he?"

"Where are Tracker and Growler?"

"How would I know? I ditched you all as soon as I could last night, remember? Those losers are probably still sleeping it off."

"I stayed at the campground up across the highway. Streamin said something about bunking at the hostel. I guess it was the same one Moonbeam and Hardware were staying in. Still, I'm surprised he hasn't shown up yet." Then he slapped his forehead. "Wait, of course! Streamin said he was going to talk to the police, remember? We agreed to wait for him."

"Well, I'm not waiting. Streamin made such a big deal about me going to the police station, I decided to meet him there. Not that I know anything that would help with their investigation. Anyway, it was a total waste of my time since he wasn't there." She was exasperated. "I'm getting out of here. It's supposed to rain soon."

Alain listened, intrigued. Given how adamant she'd been about it at dinner about not going to the farm, he was surprised she showed up at all. Still, he couldn't fault her for being uncomfortable about being a single woman alone on the trail with a murderer a few miles away. He could already tell he was going to learn a lot more this morning.

Lana Lang flagged down the waitress and ordered a black coffee. "Separate checks," she barked. "I'm giving them five more minutes, then I'm splitting. It's going to be a zoo around here."

"Sure thing, sweetie." She rolled her eyes for the benefit of the cashier, who happened to be looking up from her texting. She rolled hers back in solidarity.

Lana Lang picked up the flyer lying on their table and immediately registered her disapproval. "How is anyone supposed to know who this is, when they blocked out the face?" she asked.

She was still looking it over when Becky flipped on the television mounted on the back wall. The volume had been set high the day before, and when the news channel came on the sudden blaring caught everyone off-guard. Lana Lang registered her annoyance by covering her ears and scrunching her face, and Becky struggled to find the right button on the remote to adjust the volume. With the sound turned back to normal Lana Lang glanced back up at the television and looked surprised to see William de Beaumont staring back at her from the screen, his name captioned below the photo of his face.

She looked back down at Gear Guy's newspaper and stared at the front page for a minute, then back up at the television.

"Oh, I guess you didn't hear about the billionaire who's missing on the Appalachian Trail," said Gear Guy. "Everyone's talking about him, and they wonder if he's the same person as the dead guy on this flyer." He slid the front section across the table for her to see. "Have you heard of him?"

"I thought we were leaving," she snapped.

Gear Guy convinced her to give the others a little more time, reminding her it had been a late night for everyone. Her first cup of coffee came. Then the second. When Gear Guy left to use the Men's Room, she scooped up the flyer and newspaper and stuffed them in her backpack. Then she began fidgeting. Alain noticed her looking down at her lap every minute or so, and he could tell she was checking her watch. It was as though she expected the time to change radically, minute to minute.

The television talking head announced they were switching to a press briefing in progress with the GeoFibre Foundation president, Suzen Morova. She said the Sunday before her boss stopped on the trail approximately nine miles south of Harpers Ferry, which corresponded with his itinerary. His plan was to set up camp and continue hiking the next morning. She explained that everything was going according to plan. In fact, he was ahead of schedule.

A reporter shot up his hand. "It's been widely reported Mr. de Beaumont was a stickler for procedures. How could you lose…?"

Suzen interrupted. "Let's get something straight right away. Mr. de Beaumont IS a stickler for procedures. Not WAS. Until we find out something to the contrary, we consider him very much alive."

"I stand corrected," said the reporter. Then he asked his question again. "So, how could you lose track of him? Did somebody get sloppy?"

Sloppy was not a word in the vocabulary at GeoFibre, Suzen insisted, as she continued to spin. No, instead, a chain of unusual events allowed a lapse in monitoring. They were still reviewing their logs to find out exactly what went wrong in the process. The reporter asked for a clarification.

"Let's call it a glitch," said Suzen, offering to take one final question.

It was the one thought that was on everyone's mind. "Was there any reason to connect his disappearance with the body they recently found on the trail?"

"No, none whatsoever," she responded, and with that she thanked everyone for coming and concluded the briefing.

Lana Lang raised her hand like the reporter asking her question. "Hey! Can we go now? I don't give a crap about some idiot French guy."

"He's not French. He's Swiss," Alain corrected from his booth.

"Who cares?" she mumbled back without looking. "Sounds like he's dead now, anyway."

The bell tinkled the arrival of someone new and Growler loomed large in the doorway. He wore cheap dark and quickly walked over to join Gear Guy and Lana Lang.

"Nice shades, Growler, but where's that ugly scarf?" Gear Guy said with a laugh. "Is this your disguise to hide from all those women chasing you?"

"What are you doing here?" he asked Lana Lang, who ignored his question and called for a refill. "And where's everyone else?"

"What do you mean?" asked Gear Guy. "Aren't Tracker and Streamin with you?" Growler pleaded guilty to not knowing a thing. He guessed they were still asleep.

Lana Lang had enough. "I told you so," she grumbled. She ordered the waitress to make her another coffee to go and announced to the other two she was leaving. She said if anyone wanted to join her, they could, and if the others were smart enough to remember the name of the farm, maybe they would show up eventually, too. She didn't care. Growler managed to get her to wait long enough for him to get a coffee.

"You've got two minutes," she snapped and marched up to the cashier to pay her check. Gear Guy followed her. While she was using the restroom and out of earshot, Growler ordered the menu's special Lumberjack Breakfast of eggs, toast, hash browns and ham. "Make that to go," he added gruffly.

Growler felt annoyed Lana Lang was rushing him, and he tried to do too many things at the same time. He held his coffee in his left hand while he fished around in his jacket pocket for money with his right. It was awkward. His pocket was so crammed with stuff, when he finally managed to yank out a loose twenty-dollar bill he didn't notice the large wad of cash he pulled out at the same time. When it spilled to the floor the wad fanned out to reveal a few hundred dollars in crisp tens and twenties. He still oblivious to his loss as he walked back to the table.

"Hey, Donald Trump!" came the wise-cracking voice of Becky. "You just dropped all this. Don't know about you, but we all work pretty hard for our money around here these days." Growler sat watching her pick it all up and pile it on her serving tray. She stormed across the room and plopped the tray down on his table. "What? I have to pick it up and deliver it, too?"

If Growler wanted to attract more attention to himself, he couldn't have done a better job than he did with this spectacle in front of the restaurant full of customers. Mumbling a faint thank you, he pressed a bill into Becky's hand.

"Wow. A whole dollar! Gee, thanks! At least we know you're not that missing billionaire."

The other couple burst into laughter, and Growler didn't understand the joke.

"I'll explain later," said Gear Guy.

Growler doubled down and gave her another dollar. As he slung his backpack over his shoulder he heard the cashier's loud announcement, "Leon, your order is ready!"

Growler knocked over his chair as he raced to the cashier. He couldn't believe he had absent-mindedly given her his real name, and he wanted to be sure he got to her before she repeated it and attracted more unwanted attention.

"Leon?" snickered Lana Lang. "Leon? Your name is Leon?"

As the cashier handed him his take out, the bell jingled again and everyone looked up to see a man and a woman in uniform walk in. Growler's face turned white. He dropped the Styrofoam takeout box on the counter and whispered to the cashier that he'd be right back. Then walked nonchalantly toward the kitchen. When he got to the swinging doors, he quickly slipped right in. Before anyone noticed, Growler was out the back door.

The two officers made a quick survey of the room as they took their seats at a table in the window. "Becky, can we have some of your famous coffee, please?"

When Growler didn't come right back, Lana Lang called over to the cashier. "Hey, where did Leon go?" Without looking up, the cashier indicated the direction of the kitchen with her thumb, and Lana Lang stormed through the double doors. She returned seconds later without him and announced she was leaving. She grabbed her backpack and headed for the door, leaving Gear Guy at the table.

"Hey, wait for me!" he yelled as he gathered his things, and ran to pay his bill. While he stood in line, he casually glanced around the room, and just as it became his turn, he saw the man who had participated so much in the conversation earlier. The man turned to face him.

"Mr. Hill?"

Alain de Beaumont nodded and motioned that it was okay for Gear Guy to get on his way.

"Okay, see you around," said Gear Guy, and he hustled back over to Lana Lang, already halfway out the door.

"Hey, I just ran into Mr. Hill."

"Yeah, who cares?"

"Well, what about Growler?"

"What about him?"

Tinkle, slap, tinkle.

21

The large slanted cat's eyes of the kitchen clock darted from left to right in sync with its sequined pendulum tail. Nine o'clock. It was hardly the six am departure she planned, but Moonbeam was hungover. The head pounding was a first for her, and an inauspicious start to her day, but they were both delighted to find the hostel provided breakfast. At least now they wouldn't have to stop somewhere else and add to the delay.

The owners were in the next room when they entered the kitchen. Often, the owners didn't even realize they had guests until they heard water running in the bathroom in the morning. But this woman had been there for several days already, first with one man, and now as a couple with this new person.

In the twenty years or so they'd owned the little Shenandoah Hostel, plenty of hikers had passed through their kitchen, but none like these two. They couldn't believe the number of piercings on this young man's face, ears and neck. They knew they'd be giggling for years over others he might be sporting in places they couldn't see. No wonder he called himself Hardware.

Their appearance was only the half of it. The girl with the multicolored hair, who called herself Moonbeam, sat at the table with her head in her hands. She complained of a terrible headache, yet she babbled on incessantly. Now and then she would stop and look up. Then she would shake her head to say how the night before she had been a very bad girl, and Hardware had been a very bad boy. Sensing an endless waste of the morning, the owners made excuses and headed for their private apartment.

"Hey, wait!" Moonbeam called out. "Do you know if the trail is back open?"

"Back open?" We didn't know it was closed."

It was only a short hike down High Street to just above Shenandoah. There they found the turn to the steps leading up to St. Peter's Catholic Church and the entrance to the Appalachian Trail. From the church, the view of the Shenandoah River was as breathtaking as she'd read. At that early hour they had to admire the church's lovely stained glass windows from the outside, however. St. Peter's wouldn't open until later. Instead of a tour of the inside, Moonbeam forced a smile in an outdoor selfie to commemorate their stop. They agreed to sit and enjoy the view a little longer. At least long enough for the aspirin to kick in. After thirty minutes or so her headache abated, and they decided it was time to take on the infamous sixty-four steps up to Jefferson Rock.

At about twenty steps and off to the right they saw the charred brick ruins of St. John's Episcopal Church. With no roof, no door, and three and a half walls, it was a church that would always be open to visitors. They left the steps and walked the short distance to peek through one of the carefully restored brick rectangles that had once been a window. Then they followed the wall around to the entrance at the far end and onto the grassy, mud-packed ground that once served as the nave's floor.

Moonbeam remembered reading that the town used the church as a barracks and hospital during the Civil War. Now feeling much better, she closed her eyes and wandered the roofless remains in a sort of meditative trance. Through a series of single syllables, long pauses and humming she revealed to Hardware that she was picking up its energy.

"Yes, yes. I can feel the suffering." She walked a little farther before stopping abruptly. "Yes. I'm picking up the pain." She continued her walking meditation, making random turns. "Now I can feel...oops! Crap!" Her ethereal connection was interrupted when she stepped on a pile of feces. She begged Hardware to come to her rescue, and he helped scrape off the offending material with a sharp stick he fashioned with his virgin pocketknife. The odor was fierce, and she wanted to know what it was. She rummaged around in her backpack to retrieve one of the guidebooks and quickly identified the little mound of defecation as *Odocoileus virginianus* — deer poop.

"Typically, the pellets will clump to form a solid scat," she read aloud from the book.

For Moonbeam, stepping in deer poop seemed a small price to pay for scoring such a deep connection to the fallen soldiers of the Civil War. She turned her back to Hardware so he could replace the field guide in the designated pocket, and doing so, noticed what looked like pieces of paper on the ground a little farther away.

"Litter," she sniffed. "We've got to pick it up."

Finding any amount of litter was rare on the Appalachian Trail, as she'd learned from the literature. *Leave No Trace!* was one of the mantras of the whole trail system. One could see it everywhere, on postcards and stamped onto many souvenirs back at the Visitor Center. It referred to a set of ethics that promoted stewardship of the outdoors. That included minimizing the impact of campfires and disposing of waste properly on the trail.

As she reached down to pick up the first piece, she caught the familiar pungent smell again. On the ground in front of them they saw another pile of solid scat. But it was very different. This time it would not be necessary to consult a guidebook for identification. Wads of toilet paper scattered around like litter left no room for doubt.

She knew just where to find the camp shovel. After unfolding it and snapping it in place, Hardware reluctantly dug a few angled cuts into the ground and pried up the sod. They took turns kicking some human's number two and the toilet paper into the deep slits he'd made. Then they stomped the divot back down and refolded the shovel. She was glad they'd asked to be shown how to do it the day before in the Visitor Center.

"What kind of person would have left this mess? Certainly, not a hiker." As they we're leaving a couple of seconds later, she had her answer. Crumpled into a ball next to a wall lay Growler's ugly scarf.

"What number were we on, do you remember?" asked Moonbeam, as they resumed their hike up the steps.

Hardware was just starting to answer when the flapping wings of a large and menacing bird swooped close and startled him. He ducked and dove to the ground. Another bird circled low and threatening off to the left in the direction of Jefferson Rock. Hardware estimated its wingspan at close to two meters, and he swore he heard the birds hissing. Before he had time to dig out the field guide again, there were at least three more raptors flapping around. Moonbeam heard more behind her, and she squealed in delight. *Cathartes aura,* turkey vultures, the book read. The photos and descriptions were unmistakable.

"See? All those years of not eating meat. I told you it would all come back to me." Moonbeam had read something about animals feeling safe in the presence of vegetarians. "I mean look at all the nature I've manifested already today!"

Hardware told Moonbeam he had to take a leak and he'd meet her up at the rock. When she reached the top of the steps she saw the rustic Park Service sign with its lengthy but urgent inscription.

"Welcome to Jefferson Rock, listed on the National Registry of Historic Places. Danger! Jefferson Rock is Unstable. Walking on, climbing, ascending, descending or traversing Jefferson Rock or its supporting base rock is prohibited [36 CFR 2.A (A) (5)]"

Ignoring the warning, she walked closer for a better view of the gleaming flat slab of shale. It stretched majestically atop four little red sandstone pillars, which in turn rested upon the largest in a pile of boulders. But it was not the formation or the otherwise stunning view that would be etched in her memory forever. That honor went to the thing wedged into a shallow crevice on one side, being feasted upon by six or eight frenzied vultures. This time, no field guide was necessary. Tattered blue-jeans indicated exactly what kind of mammal stared back.

Homo sapiens sapiens.

22

Gear Guy had to hustle to keep up with her. It wasn't that she'd set such a fast pace. He just found it a little early in the day to be so energetic. A police car from some jurisdiction or another turned toward town from the highway. As soon as it passed she quickened her speed. Finally, when she stopped briefly at an intersection, he managed to ask her a question.

"Shouldn't we wait for Growler!"

"You can. I'm not," she said in her typical brusque style. "I want to get out of this place."

Gear Guy pressed her. "Come on, aren't you the least bit curious why he left in such a hurry?"

"Look, are you stupid? The cops came. He split. Do the math." She turned back around and then winced. Her hand went quickly to the back of her head. "Somebody just threw a rock or something at me."

"Not a rock, a beer can." Gear Guy spotted the hunk of crumpled aluminum on the ground behind her. "I'll bet it was that."

"Psst, Lana Lang. Over here!" They both spun around to see Growler waving his arms from his hiding place behind a dumpster. He asked if the coast was clear. She gave him the finger and took off up the road again.

Gear Guy yelled over to him. "I can see the highway just up ahead. Hurry up."

Growler tiptoed out from behind the dumpster, checking to see if the coast was clear, and ran to catch up.

When they reached the highway, it was Growler's idea to use Lana Lang as bait for a ride, and he gave her an awkward demonstration how to stick her thumb out and look sexy.

"I know how to hitchhike, you moron."

Growler sniffed at the rebuke, but let it go. He was in a hurry, and he dashed into the weeds alongside the road with Gear Guy to hide from view. While they were squatting down, his stomach growled again, and he asked Gear Guy if he had by any chance grabbed his take-out. He was hungry.

"No, but what the hell, Growler? What's the matter with you? Are you running from the cops or something?"

Fortunately for Growler, he didn't have to respond, because Lana Lang and her thumb were successful in attracting a ride. A beat up maroon pickup pulled over quickly and slowed to a stop. Its back bumper and tailgate were plastered with *South of the Border* stickers.

"Where to, little lady?" shouted the driver through the half-open passenger window.

"You heard of a place called Ridgefield Farm?" Just then, several squad cars whizzed past them, and the screaming of their sirens made it impossible for him to hear her question. High intensity flashing lights from their roof racks added another layer of chaos and distraction. The truck driver cupped a hand around his ear and asked her to repeat.

"I'm going to Ridgefield Farm," she yelled, over the noise. "Do you know where it is?"

Another speeding police car and then another joined in the wailing and the flashing. They came from all directions, but they were headed to the same place, Harpers Ferry. The strobes were blinding, and the noise deafening. Finally, the driver gave up trying to hear her, and reached across the cab and opened the passenger door.

Growler and Gear Guy bolted from their hiding spot and all three tossed their things into the truck bed. Lana Lang and Growler pushed and shoved to see who could get in the cab first. Lana Lang claimed the front seat, leaving Gear Guy to squeeze into the back of the cab with Growler. Without checking to see if he was completely inside, she slammed the passenger door shut, nearly crushing Gear Guy's foot. Instantly, there was quiet.

"Jesus, what's the big hurry?" he complained.

The driver knew exactly how to get to Ridgefield Farm. He passed it every day and said he hoped it would be all right to drop them off at the entrance. His rough complexion was littered with scars, and a well-worn cowboy hat sat atop a thick blond mop of hair. He told them they were very lucky he picked them up when he did, since he heard the law wasn't going to let anyone in or out of Harpers Ferry for a while. Then he laughed.

"The name's Frank. So which one of you is the missing billionaire?"

Lana Lang told him he was dead.

"Oh, is that the guy they found? No wonder there are so many cop cars." Frank wanted to know what else they knew, and Gear Guy gave him a quick recap of the victim – a tall guy with a beard, probably early thirties.

"But my friend here is wrong. Nobody confirmed the victim was the billionaire."

Frank said he'd heard the man's neck was snapped and everything. "Got any other details?"

Gear Guy added a little more about the victim's tent and confirmed that the police were calling it a homicide. "We got the story last night, straight from a police scanner."

"Huh? What do you mean last night?"

"Like I said, we heard it at dinner, at the White Horse."

"Sorry guys, that's impossible. First, are you sure you mean the White Horse? That place has been out of business for months. Anyway, they just found the dead guy this morning, so I'd say you heard that wrong, too."

"No, it was definitely the White Horse. I remember we…"

Lana Lang piped in. "It has to be the same person. How many dead bodies could there be on the Appalachian Trail in one day? But I want to know why they would close Harpers Ferry, considering they found the body up at some shelter named Shady Pines."

"The Shady Pines shelter?" Frank sounded incredulous. "No, no. Wrong again, I'm afraid. Or we're talking about two different people. The dead person I'm talking about a couple of hikers found right here in Harpers Ferry, up at Jefferson Rock."

"What?!" Gear Guy stuck his ashen face into the front seat.

Frank said he hoped he was mistaken, and he'd call his wife to straighten it out. When a woman somewhere answered on the truck's speakerphone, he got right to the point.

"Honey, didn't you tell me it was Harpers Ferry where they found the body this morning? I'm with some hikers who are telling me a completely different story. They said there was a dead body at Shady Pines campground. "Which one is it?"

"My stars, Frank. Both. It's all over the news. There was the one at the Shady Pines Shelter last night. That was apparently from a few days ago. And this morning, they found another one, up at Jefferson Rock. I swear I told you at breakfast."

Gear Guy panicked. "Oh, my god. Another murder. Hey Frank, ask her if she has a description of the person they found this morning. I'm worried it could be a friend of ours."

"Who is with you? Am I on your speakers? Listen to me, Frank, a big thunderstorm is on the way, so I need you stop at the store and pick up some milk and toilet paper, okay? Oh, and promise me you won't pick up any more hitchhikers on the way. There's a madman loose around here."

Frank took the call off speaker and mumbled that the hikers were just getting out. As soon as everyone grabbed their gear, he floored it and sped off in a spray of gravel, leaving the passenger door still open and flapping. The truck was over a hill and out of sight in seconds.

"He didn't even wait for us to thank him for the ride," said Gear Guy staring at the empty road. When he turned around, he discovered he'd been talking to himself. Lana Lang and Growler were already heading down the farm's long driveway.

When he caught up to them, Growler asked him if he knew who they were supposed to see about the jobs.

"What do you mean, the jobs? You aren't serious about staying here after what we just heard? We've got to go back. Somebody got killed at Jefferson Rock last night, and it might be one of our friends."

Lana Lang was dismissive. "Look, they weren't my friends. I just met them. Anyway, why would anyone want to kill a couple of idiot nobodies like Tracker or Streamin?"

"I'm not going all the way back there," said Growler. "They were both alive when I left. I'm sure they're fine."

Gear Guy was in a hurry to return to town, but he didn't want to give up on persuading them to come along. As he walked backwards toward the entrance he made his last attempt at cheerleading. "So, who's coming with me, huh?"

Honk! Honk! The driver of the speeding car slammed on the horn and swerved to avoid hitting him. He had become so emotional he hadn't noticed he was already standing in the road. Startled by the blare, he lurched to one side and fell into a drainage ditch. The pool of standing water where he landed was deep enough to get him soaked, but he wasn't hurt. He was discouraged, though, seeing Lana Lang and Growler walking on ahead towards the farmhouse.

It was starting to mist. And according to Frank's wife, it would be raining hard very soon.

23

<Are you sitting down?

>Uh, oh.

<We just connected some new dots. No way to sugar coat this, friend. The assassin you're looking for down there really is Le Mauvais. Sorry.

>Not surprised when you look at both bodies side by side. The technique was unmistakable.

<How can we help?

>I want to get him this time. A detailed description would be nice. All the guys in the group are at least six feet tall and look alike.

<Wish we could give you something. He's probably wearing a disguise anyway.

>Speaking of that, I decided to ditch the wig. Doesn't fit very well anymore.

<Ha-ha. It never did.

24

"WORKERS THIS WAY" read the hand-painted wooden sign driven into the ground on a flimsy stake. It was at the end of the farm's thinly graveled driveway and pointed to the back of one of the barns. There, next to a heavy old wooden picnic table, stood a tall scarecrow with a smiling face drawn with a magic marker on a pumpkin head. Both of its hands pointed to the table. Another sign read, "Hikers wait here."

"Oh, great," groused Lana Lang. "Another *hiker table*."

They didn't have to wait long before an ancient and rusty one-eyed Land Rover rumbled around from the other side of the barn. The sound of squeaky brakes accompanied an impressive backfire and a cloud of black smoke, as it slammed to a stop in front of their table. The dented driver's side door let out a screech when it opened, and a young Hispanic with straight, shiny black shoulder length hair bounded out.

Remaining seated, Growler took charge. "We're here for a job," he stated confidently. "Who are we supposed to see?"

Ninety seconds of rapid-fire Spanish disarmed Growler immediately, and he was reduced to a weak protest. "Me no habla Spanish!"

Unfazed, the Hispanic pointed to their gear and motioned for them to follow. When they stopped at a clearing, the Hispanic pointed at the gathering storm clouds and started speaking Spanish again, accompanying it with wild animated gestures. Growler complained the guy was speaking even faster this time, and looked over to Lana Lang for empathy. "Can you believe this guy?" He shrugged. "Now what are we supposed to do?"

"You dope. He told us to pitch our tents over near the outhouse. He said some other stuff, too."

"Wait, you speak Spanish? Why didn't you say so up there?"

"God, you are such a loser!" she snapped.

The Hispanic faced Growler and pointed to a spot about twenty feet away. "Tents," he said. "You put."

The farm's shabby condition wasn't exactly what Growler expected. The clearing was in the remains of a large and decrepit garden about thirty yards by a hundred. Patchwork fencing surrounded it on three sides. Some chicken wire here, and some checkerboard style deer fencing there. Weeds had overtaken the raised beds, and morning glories strangled the chicken wire. At one end sat a tumbled down shack, that was probably once an old chicken coop. Next to it was an old-fashioned hand pump.

"What's the password for the Wi-Fi?" asked Lana Lang in Spanish.

More Spanish from the Hispanic explained there wasn't a strong signal where they were, but she could pick it up closer to the house. She would have to get the password from the boss. He excused himself and walked back to the car.

"Did you ask him about the Wi-Fi?"

"Of course. He wouldn't give the password to me, but it'll only take me two minutes to hack. It will be something dumb like *farm*. Even you should be able to figure it out."

"Hey, the good thing is we're off the trail and away from all the cops," said Growler.

Lana Lang said she wasn't a fan of the cops much either, but at least she wasn't running from them. Growler asked her if the Mexican said anything about getting paid. She told him they were going to get two hundred dollars a day. And Alvaro was Chilean, not Mexican, she corrected.

"Whatever." He was thrilled. Two hundred a day was a lot of money, and he hoped that didn't mean the work would be too hard, especially since the mist had turned to a sprinkle.

Lana Lang went to a spot in the far corner of the clearing to make her camp, and her tent was up in minutes. She positioned it for maximum privacy, with the zippered door flap facing away from the center of the space. Growler carried his stuff over and plopped down next to her.

"Find your own spot!" she barked through the flap, shooing him away. "I don't want you anywhere near me."

Unfazed, he dragged his gear back away from her to a spot on the other side of the outhouse. There he let out a long series of expletives. He was really getting tired of her attitude, but it wasn't Lana Lang he was cursing. It was about having to set up his tent, always his least favorite thing to do. And now it had begun to rain.

"Hey, since it's raining, do you think we'll still get paid?" If Lana Lang heard him, she didn't answer.

Growler fumbled around with his tent, and his non-proficiency had little to do with the rain. The tent had met the same fate as every other piece of gear he bought that day. He barely took the time to pull things out of the boxes they came in before cramming them in his crappy little backpack. In his haste, he threw away the instructions along with the packaging.

The metal stakes were like his tent — flimsy and cheap. Using a rock as a hammer, he managed to snap two of them in half the first night. The ones that didn't break, bent. Early on he broke one of the tent poles, too, when he carelessly shoved it back into his pack too fast and too hard, and since then the tent listed to one side and sagged in the middle. To make matters worse, it only took him zipping and unzipping the front flap twice, before it stuck in the unzipped position. Not to mention, it was way too small for a man his size. He probably should have listened to the salesman.

Buying his camping gear came down to about twenty tense minutes in a big box store not too far away in southwestern Pennsylvania. A young sales associate said Growler was lucky, because he was a hiker, too, and he could give him some serious product advice. What Growler was though, was impatient, and he didn't have time to listen to recommendations.

"So, what do you need?" asked the salesman.

"Everything."

The teenager laughed a little. "I'm sure that's not true. Let's start with what you have."

"I don't have anything."

The potential of this sale had the kid glad he was on commission. They would start with the tent, and he motioned for Growler to follow him to another aisle. When they arrived at the shelves of tents, he found far more styles and sizes than he ever cared to know about. The associate wanted to talk about the climate and terrain Growler would encounter, but he ignored him. He grabbed the first tent he saw and threw it into his shopping cart. It was on sale for $39.95.

"I want the cheapest one." He was emphatic, and it became the standard rebuttal to almost every item the salesman suggested.

The young man said he wanted to show Growler some other essential items. "You'll need a tarp, a cook set, and a canteen. They're over in aisle twenty-eight." When Growler asked him what a cook set was, the young man's response belied his astonishment. "You know, pots and pans."

"Pots and pans? Are you kidding? I'm not going to be cooking."

The associate was confused but his customer was becoming testy, and he didn't want to lose the sale. Growler resented having to go back and forth between sections. He'd already been there ten minutes, and he still needed to buy clothes, so he told the kid just to go ahead and pick out the rest of the stuff without him. He said he'd be right back.

"But what time of the year are you going?" the kid asked. "Because it really matters, if..."

Growler, already halfway down the aisle, turned and yelled back. "Today. Now. I'm leaving as soon as we're done!"

Another delay. He spotted a couple of store security guards and had to make a long detour. When he got back to the camping department with a couple extra T-shirts, some socks and a cheap hooded sweatshirt, he found the young man had done his job. Growler's cart was full. He snapped at the kid. "How am I supposed to carry all this?"

The kid smiled back tentatively and held out the backpack he'd selected. One look at the price tag and Growler shoved it right back. His eyes went straight to the cheapest one and he yanked it off the shelf. Without a word of thanks to the helpful clerk, he wheeled his cart off down the aisle.

On the way to checkout he tossed about half the items onto random shelves and into bins of other merchandise. A First Aid kit and a compass? What was the kid thinking? A hatchet? He wasn't planning on chopping wood. It landed in a bin of ladies' lingerie. One of the things he did keep was the headlamp. The boy said they were great for hiking at night, and he was a little surprised Growler would be interested in it. At check out, he threw a dozen candy bars and a few bags of chips onto the conveyor belt.

"Sign here, please," said the cashier. To Growler's relief the credit card went through. When he exited the store, he decided not to press his luck any further, and dropped it into a trashcan.

Long ago he'd learned the skills to avoid being captured on store security cameras, so head down, he hustled to the far end of the parking lot. As soon as he got in the dented Mercedes, that week's ride, he started stuffing his purchases in the backpack. Fitting everything in was frustrating. He still had too much stuff, so he dumped a few things out the car window. Twenty miles later he was out of the city limits. The car's navigation system led him to one of the paths connecting the Appalachian Trail to the highway. He locked the car, and as he entered the trail, he tossed the keys into the woods.

From the very first step he took, he knew he had made a mistake. Even after dumping so many things his new backpack felt horribly heavy. After five minutes the path went up a little ridge and the hike became strenuous and not fun at all. In ten minutes, he was dying of thirst. It was going to be far worse than he'd imagined, but somehow, he needed to figure out a way to endure it for a month or so. By then maybe he would be out of the woods. Literally, and figuratively.

Distance was never his objective. His goal was to keep moving and stay out of sight. After two and a half weeks on the trail he'd covered a lot of miles, but hadn't gone far. Since he hadn't thought to pick up a map, and he'd tossed the compass onto a bin of toilet brushes, he ended up going back and forth without realizing it. He started out heading north, but after the second night he forgot which direction he was going and ended up going south. To avoid being seen he decided to hike at night and sleep by day, using shelters when he could. When he found a good one, he might stay a couple nights. A good shelter had nothing to do with its condition or its facilities or its view. A good one had no other hikers using it, and he hated when one was occupied. That meant he had to set up his tent.

Not thinking through the food situation was his biggest mistake. He'd never been in a park that didn't have a snack bar before, and he figured he would just buy food along the way. He remembered the look on the faces of the first hikers when he asked them how far to the nearest concession stand. It was a rude awakening to learn hikers cooked their own food. Apparently, it was supposed to be part of the adventure, part of the fun. Pots and pans.

Leaving the trail during the day to eat really interfered with his sleep. Some of the closest stores were many miles off the Trail. And, each time he left it, he ran the risk of being seen. He found it was easier to bum food from other hikers by making up stories about how animals raided his supplies. After a week, he had developed quite a repertoire of practiced lies.

He was surveying his work when he spotted Lana Lang entering the outhouse. He had to hand it to her; she was braver than him. No way would he ever set foot in there. Anyway, as it turned out, he preferred pooping in the woods.

25

"Esther Blankenship. Man-o-man what a mess! She's the one with all the men? She certainly was a plain Jane when she worked here."

It took no time at all for the GeoFibre HR Department to find Moonbeam's employment record and her real identity. The woman only worked at GeoFibre six months before the company had to terminate her for repeated and unwanted sexual advances. No one could believe it. She promptly sued, but it was her subsequent rap for prostitution during litigation that got them off the hook.

"Tornado was right about the plastic surgery. One of her co-workers recalled she was fairly flat-chested and a little homely back then. He added that Esther bragged to everyone on her way out that her grandmother had just died and left her fifty-thousand dollars, and she didn't care that she got fired."

"Thanks, Suzen. That could explain where she got the money for all the plastic surgery. I don't know if it's relevant, but it's all grist for the mill."

She called to give an update on the computer sabotage. Her engineers concluded that someone introduced the virus to the controlling server with a simple thumb drive. The server was housed in an underutilized facility in western Maryland, only twenty or thirty miles from Harpers Ferry, and while the location and facility were not secret, whoever was responsible for the sabotage could only have known about its existence by inside knowledge.

The culprit also had to know of a security camera for the building, because it had been disabled. On that point, Suzen said the company lucked out, because what the felon didn't know, was that a brand-new camera system had recently been installed. The new one was undetectable, and while it was being tested, the previous camera was still operative. Since they knew exactly when the break in occurred, it wouldn't take the team long to find some usable film.

"So, by what you've told me, it appears one guy could have done it all. Our server is so close to where I am now, he could have sabotaged our computer on the way to the trail. Listen to me. I've been saying *he* all the time. Do you think it Esther Blankenship could have learned the location of the server?"

"I doubt that very much, but we'll soon see. We're combing through the footage as we speak."

"Please hurry. I'm eager to learn if your image will match with any of the suspects we have contained at the farm. I'm arranging to bring the others out later today, but I can't keep them here forever. Tonight's picnic should shake somebody loose."

"Don't you think all signs still point to that Growler guy, don't they? It's seems pretty obvious to me with his record and all."

The only two from dinner that the FBI could identify were Hardware and Growler. Hardware was a Serbian citizen, as Alain had guessed from his accent. The only reason they had his prints,

147

was because he'd agreed to provide them to Customs and Immigration when he entered the United States. Otherwise, he was clean. Alain thought it a bit odd that Hardware so overtly declined to let Tracker see his Epix watch up close. But then he recalled Lucky's arrival interrupted the conversation, and the request wasn't allowed to play out.

"I'm sorry our guys haven't been able to fix the computer system yet. I'd like to be able to show you where all his gear and clothing ended up."

It would be so easy to use the information their tracking system collected to reconstruct the chain of events. At the very least, it could clear up some speculation, and Alain was frustrated that the data was still inaccessible.

"And you're right about Growler. He's a prosecutor's dream, with a list of crimes and misdemeanors and aliases the length of my arm. On the face of it he'd be somebody the cops would likely want to run in and question. I honestly wonder if he's smart enough to be the crack assassin who had eluded Interpol and me and every other agency for years. I don't know, I guess it's possible he may just be a good actor."

From every outward manifestation, the rest of them seemed to be just good guys. Gear Guy seemed innocent enough, for example, except for the one thing that set him apart from the others. Not only did he know a lot about François, he seemed overly interested in him, almost to the point of obsession. He had that passion for GeoFibre, too. So, until Alain learned something to exclude him from the list, Gear Guy would remain a suspect with the others.

Tornado was still trying to mine information from the other two hikers he'd found and befriended. While neither manifested anything outward that would draw undue suspicion, like Streamin and Gear Guy, the two weren't traveling together, and the agency had proved time and again the adage that lone wolves make viable suspects.

Though he didn't know where it might lead, Alain wanted to double down on finding Lana Lang's missing boyfriend...if there was one. It was hard for him to imagine someone being attracted to her, as unpleasant as she had been at dinner. He considered that maybe she was just having a bad day and was tired of sitting around waiting for the guy. After all, she did show a softer side when she surprised everyone by making that generous donation to the animal shelter. Apart from not admitting to seeing Hardware on the sly, Lana Lang didn't strike him as dishonest – quite the opposite. Still, the alleged boyfriend's character was an unknown, and thus far he was the only wild card they had.

"But how can you ask anyone to search for someone without giving them a name or a face? How would you even think outside the box on this one?"

"I don't expect them to. And Suzen, now that you are working with us on this project, it's time you learned my way of problem-solving. It's no longer thinking inside or outside of a box. It's not having a box at all."

26

Lana Lang held her phone inside her rain slicker, but kept it unzipped so she could watch the Wi-Fi signal strength icon. It was raining lightly, but she didn't mind. Like a rat going through an invisible maze, she zig-zagged the quarter mile or so to the house, tracing the changes in signal strength. She would pause briefly and then turn for a few feet, stop and turn again. Finally, she stopped under the thick protection of an old maple tree in the side yard next to a barn and leaned against its smooth trunk. Her fingers flew over her keypad. "Ha!" she muttered after only a few minutes. "*Farm123.* I knew it!"

Then she slipped into the barn, just in time, too, because the earlier steady rain suddenly became torrential. Once inside she entered the door Alvaro described, which led, as promised, to the interior accommodations. On either side of the narrow hallway were small motel-like bedrooms, each complete with a television. None were occupied, so she selected the room with the strongest Wi-Fi signal. The outlet next to the bed was a plus, too. Now she could keep her phone charged while she relaxed, and she could catch up on the email she missed since logging in at the Hiker Lounge.

She did a quick check of the weather. The unprecedented amount of rain they were experiencing was the backlash of a hurricane that had torn up parts of the Virginia coast. On her way to the barn, she let out a giggle at Growler's pitiful setup. His tent had already collapsed, and his feet were sticking out the door flap. He must have been completely soaked, and the rain had only begun. It was expected to continue through the night.

Before she logged off, she visited her social media accounts and was checking her news feed when one post caught her eye. It looked like an ad she'd probably ignored a dozen times, but it wasn't an ad. It was one of those local news items that got served to your feed based on your location. Now that she was taking her time and not scrolling so fast, the photo popped out at her. *Share if you have seen this man.* The story was about a tragic hit and run which left a child severely injured, and the mugshot of the alleged driver of the car was a very familiar face.

27

At the end of a day of one failed experiment after another, they found themselves up against a brick wall, and most of the team decided to pack it in for the day. Dr. Lambiel, the lead scientist, had just finished putting the arcane device back together for the night when his lab assistant stopped by on her way out. She knew her boss felt frustrated, and she offered to pass on some advice given to her by her grandfather, also a famous scientist. When he couldn't find the solution to a problem, he used the 'out of sight, out of mind' strategy.

"He meant he put the problem aside and let it go for a while," she said. "Oh, and don't forget you have that meeting over in South Lab in five minutes."

Dr. Lambiel had forgotten the meeting and thanked her for the reminder. He didn't thank her for the advice, however. Tired old sayings like the one from her grandfather rubbed him the wrong way. As he tightened the last screw on the back of the device he wished her a good evening, instead. Then he stood up and gathered his notes for the meeting. He looked at his watch, and knew he could still be on time. South Lab was an unsecured building, and he wouldn't need to spend time presenting credentials at multiple security checks, as was necessary in his part of the complex.

Everyone else in his lab had already left and closed the vault for the evening, and since he was running late he didn't want to take the time to reopen it. Instead, he dropped the gadget into his lab pocket for safe keeping and headed out the door.

The meeting had already started when the last pair of automatic doors slid apart to admit him into South Lab, and as he strode across the room to take his seat at the round table with the others he apologized profusely. He'd been so rushed and focused on offering a plausible excuse he didn't notice what everyone else heard. The other scientists assumed the offending buzzing sound came from his mobile phone he'd forgotten to silence, and they pointed at his lab coat. Dr. Lambiel jabbed his hand into his pocket and retrieved the strange device he'd forgotten he put there. Faint squawking sounds and pulsing beeps were coming from the earbuds. When he put those earbuds in his ears, the real analysis began.

Like the game where the child is told when he is getting warmer or colder, the scientist wandered around the lab following the sound to where it became the loudest.

"Voilà!" he announced, hovering around a lab bench. The setup looked like it could be in any lab anywhere. Abandoned electronics were piled high, with lots of wires connecting things to other things with alligator clips. "Can someone please tell me whose bench this is, and what they are working on?" he asked the room.

The rest of the scientists crowded around, but what they had to offer wasn't much help. The area where the gadget was making all the noise wasn't currently being used. The scientist whose bench it was quit after only working in the lab a short while. Problems with getting a security clearance, or something. He'd been gone three months at least.

"Well, something here is causing this thing to talk to me," he said, thrilled at a breakthrough.

He postponed the meeting agenda until they got to the bottom of it, with everything on the bench to be examined. One by one, each item was removed from the room systematically. When the device continued to emit noises at the same decibel level, even after the last piece of equipment had been taken, he was stumped. All that remained was a small office pencil holder, containing the usual random collection of ballpoint pens and the odd paperclip. So, one by one they removed the pens. Exasperated at the continued beeping, Dr. Lambiel tipped over the pencil holder and emptied the remaining contents onto the countertop.

A few paper clips bounced and spread out to reveal the culprit — a clothing label. And not just any label. An unused GeoFibre label coded for the personal use of William de Beaumont. When it was removed from the room, the gadget became quiet again.

By the end of the evening Dr. Lambiel had packaged the device with instructions and a new battery charger. He also inserted a brief handwritten note.

This device was made at the GeoFibre lab in right here in Montreux, but with components acquired from Russia. Within hours the device was back on a plane bound for Harpers Ferry, West Virginia, and to the hands of the man who discovered it, Alain de Beaumont.

28

Gear Guy was fuming...and worried. He was worried about the fate of his friends, Tracker and Streamin, and steamed that Lana Lang and Growler had been so callous. Terrifying thoughts and strong emotions fought for his brain's attention. *If one of them was dead, where was the other? Dead, too, or just not found yet? If neither was dead, why didn't they show up at breakfast?* His mind was speeding. So was his pace.

And then something occurred to him, and he came to an abrupt stop. For the past forty-five minutes or so, he'd been replaying possible scenarios so many times he hadn't paid attention to where he was headed, and he realized he'd been going in the wrong direction. When he pulled himself up out of the pool of water, he'd let his little temper tantrum take over and just started walking. Now he had to turn around and go all the way back to the farm and start over in the right direction. *Crap, what a waste of time!*

Doubling back to the farm was the easy part. In this brief new moment of clarity, it also occurred to him that he had no idea where he was. Not where the farm was in relation to the town, or even the name of the road he was on. He couldn't really blame himself for being uncharacteristically lost. Between the racket of those sirens and the intense conversation with the driver from his crammed spot in the back seat with Growler, he hadn't paid any attention to the turns they made.

Gear Guy was nearly back to the farm entrance when he heard the rumbling of a vehicle behind him, and he was surprised to see the same maroon pickup that had dropped them off. He stuck out his thumb, and Frank pulled over.

"Quick, hop in. I'll give you a ride, but you have to promise not to tell my wife. She'd kill me if she found out I was still picking up hitchhikers." He was back on the road, because he'd forgotten to buy toilet paper, and she'd added ammunition to the list.

Compared to the chaotic scene that morning, by noon there wasn't a cop car in sight, let alone twenty, and the town of Harpers Ferry was doornail dead. Since the few hikers his team rounded up were convinced they couldn't leave town, Alain no longer needed to put on quite the show up at the highway. One squad car would suffice to keep up the pretense of a blockade. Today he wanted to see what he could learn from the ones who were still in town, before he connived them into going to the farm with the others. With more information, and all of them in the same place, he hoped he could maneuver the assassin into revealing himself.

In the meantime, he learned that Gear Guy was safely in the truck and just entering town. He was intrigued and eager to find out why he'd left. The small plastic table chained to a post on the sidewalk outside The Beanery would be the perfect stage for the intervention. Besides, another café au lait was just what Alain needed to clear his head. He was glad he thought to pop for an elaborate coffee machine for the diner's kitchen. As often as he was planning to frequent that place, he'd need a proper cup, something that was otherwise impossible to come by in the little town.

He pretended to be talking on his phone when Gear Guy approached him. Alain gestured for him to join him at the table. He explained he needed to finish the call, but asked Gear Guy to order him a café au lait and to get whatever else he wanted.

"You look terrible, by the way, and you stink. Give me a minute, will you? I'll be right back." He chuckled as he left. After the drunken mess wino act he put on the night before, he must have appeared very sophisticated.

Gear Guy ran dirty fingers through his hair, hoping it would make him appear more presentable, and then he recalled the restaurant had a decent rest room and decided to go freshen up a bit before Mr. Hill returned. He also looked around inside for a more comfortable place to sit. His table from the morning was available, but he walked right past it and grabbed an empty booth at the front. The red naugahyde upholstery looked inviting. Posters from just about every organization and real estate agent in the county plastered the large window, but conspicuously missing was the flyer that was everywhere that morning.

He tried several times to get Becky's attention. She was the same waitress who served him in the morning, but now she seemed to ignore him, dashing past him with orders for everyone else. He waved his arms. He raised his voice.

"Excuse me, coffee?"

"I see you," she said, snapping her gum. She banged through the swinging doors back into the kitchen and never came over.

He thought he might have better luck with the cashier. She was the same one, too, and he'd done her that favor earlier. He explained he'd been waiting for quite a while and asked if it was okay to serve himself.

"Your wait staff will take your order," she clarified, without looking up from her iPhone. He gave a little sigh and walked back to his booth empty handed.

"What made you change tables?" Alain slid into the booth to join his young friend.

"Oh, man. I needed something more comfortable. My butt took quite a beating this morning." He related the story about falling into the ditch and landing on some sharp rocks.

"The booth must feel luxurious." Alain couldn't suppress another laugh. "Hey, weren't you going to order me a café au lait?"

"Sorry, Mr. Hill, I've been trying. It's like the waitress is ignoring me on purpose."

"Allow me," said Alain. He turned his head ever so slightly toward Becky and gave her a nearly imperceptible nod. As if by some magnetic force, her eyes were instantly drawn to his. Gear Guy was astonished that a minute later she returned with his café au lait, a regular coffee for himself, and two menus. He wanted to know how he did it.

Mr. Hill said, "One day maybe I'll share my secret. In the meantime, though, I thought you were off to work on a farm today. What changed your mind?"

Gear Guy took a breath. "It's a long story, but before I forget, I want to thank you for buying dinner last night. You took us all by surprise. Sorry I couldn't speak with you this morning. It was a little awkward with the others."

"Oh, I completely understand. I noticed Lana Lang was in a rush, too, but points for remembering to say thank you. Now what about that long story?"

"Yes, but I've got so much on my mind right now. First, I want to talk about the new murder I just learned about."

"Yes, the news today about Jefferson Rock was tragic, wasn't it? It's the talk of the town, of course. And on top of that other grisly murder at the shelter."

"Well, I'm going to tell you something, and I hope you'll keep it between us. After dinner, a bunch of us went up there to take in the view. It was late, but nobody was ready to turn in. Some of the guys were going to spend the night up there. Well this morning neither Tracker or Streamin showed up to go to the farm. I didn't think much of it at the time, but now I'm worried the dead person they found might be one of them."

"Oh, I see. So, you don't know who it was yet? Well, maybe I can help. Was there something else?"

"That would be great. Thanks. And yes. Remember those flyers that were everywhere this morning? They're gone now. Do you think that means somebody identified the body? Then there's this whole other thing about William de Beaumont being missing."

"Ah, yes, de Beaumont, the other talk of the town. You seem to know quite a bit about him. Something about studying him in college?"

"I did a paper on him for a business course. In fact, it's been a dream to work at a company like his one day." Then Gear Guy leaned in and whispered. "This might sound callous, Mr. Hill, because those dead bodies turning up have to be somebody's friends and relatives, but I hope they turn out to be someone else. I'd really like to see him walk in here right now. The world could use a few more de Beaumonts."

"I'd very much like to see him walk in now, myself," said Alain. He motioned for a refill and changed the subject. "Did I hear you have an MBA?"

Gear Guy said his finances hadn't permitted him to finish, but he was only short a semester. He had gotten discouraged and was using his time on the trail to sort out his next steps.

"Economics isn't always fair, that's for sure," said Alain. "But let's get back to that long tale of yours. It sounds like I left the restaurant too early and missed a lot."

Gear Guy told him the whole story beginning with how surprised everyone was to learn he'd picked up their tabs. He described how wasted Moonbeam and Hardware had been, and how they went straight to the hostel while everyone else went up to Jefferson Rock to see the view.

"What about the girl? Did she go, too?"

"Lana Lang? Oh, no, not her. She didn't want anything to do with any of us. She split about the same time as Moonbeam and Hardware. I don't know where she stayed, at the hostel, I imagine. I never asked. Tracker had the hots for her, but I sure wasn't a fan. I forgot to mention Streamin was with us, too, although he fell asleep almost as soon as we got up there."

"I hate to interrupt, but you and Streamin were friends, am I right? I remember you came into the restaurant together."

Gear Guy shrugged. "I didn't know Streamin well at all. We just happened to be hiking a part of the trail at the same time, and ended up in Harpers Ferry together. Besides, Streamin always wore his earbuds, and there was never much conversation."

Then he related the story of catching Tracker at the last minute before going off the ledge.

"Wow, you're quite the hero."

"That's what Tracker said. He promised to pay me back for it one day."

"What on earth could Tracker do for you? He doesn't appear to be someone with many resources. If he were sitting here, I'd advise him to spend some money with an orthodontist first, wouldn't you agree?"

"Tracker was probably just drunk when he said it, and you know, I really don't expect to hear from him again. But gee, like he said, I did save his life. I'd hate it if he ended up dead up there, after all."

"Let's be positive, and assume Tracker is not the one they found." Mr. Hill giggled. "Next time you see him. why don't you ask him to pay the rest of your business school tuition?"

Gear Guy got a kick out of the gag, but he wanted to change the subject back to William de Beaumont. "Can I run something past you? Let's say he's not dead, either. So, if all the hikers were taken off the trail, where is he? Shouldn't he be in town here with the rest of us?"

Just then, Becky arrived with the check, and before she could spin around to leave, Gear Guy asked her to stay. "Just out of curiosity," he asked. "Do you remember me? Because I have a question for you."

"Sure, hon. Of course I remember. You were here this morning with that unpleasant woman and the big shot with all the money, who didn't tip worth a darn."

He gulped. "Wow, that's the impression I gave?"

A B Gibson

"You are judged by the company you keep, Gear Guy," Alain cautioned, citing the famous fable of Aesop. "But fear not. Reputations can be fixed."

"Anyway, hon, was that your question? Because I'm busy."

"I noticed all the posters about the dead body in the shelter are down. Does that mean they found out who the guy was?"

"Sure does." She turned to go.

"Wait! Was it William de Beaumont?"

"The missing billionaire?" She started to clear a nearby table. "Heavens, no. Turned out to be a local guy. A poor kid with a sad story, but it's no wonder, coming from a family like his."

"Are you sure?"

"Positive."

"Then where do you suppose he is?"

"Who?"

"de Beaumont."

"I don't know. But they've got this town sealed off, so he's got to be around here somewhere."

PART THREE

29

It was raining hard when they left The Beanery. Gear Guy mentioned wanting to sleep in an actual bed for once, and he asked Mr. Hill for a lift to the hostel. When they got there, they were greeted with a NO VACANCY sign. The owners said they hadn't been this busy in years.

"Apparently, some bears scared all the hikers off the trail, and the authorities are putting everyone up in Harpers Ferry. It's always feast or famine."

They would have a bed, if the couple that left in the morning hadn't come right back. They were the ones who discovered the latest corpse, and understandably, they were still in shock. The owners felt terrible and squeezed them in again.

She lay the reservation list back down on the counter. "I'm really sorry," she said. "We don't have a single bed left." She secured it with a Jefferson Rock paperweight, as if to put the request to rest.

"What about the bunk we saved for the guy who never showed up?" asked her husband from across the room. "I don't think he's ever going to come, so I say we rent it to this guy."

Gear Guy was ecstatic. "Thank you, person who never showed up. Because of you this place will be my home, sweet home for a while."

"Things will be a lot sweeter for everyone else after you take a shower and do some laundry," joked Alain. He excused himself to take care of some pressing things. "Maybe I'll see you a little later. It's one of the niceties about a small town. People run into each other all the time."

On the way to the shower, Gear Guy dropped his dirty clothes in the washer the owners provided as a free service, because they learned long ago it was better than putting up with a hostel full of stinky hikers.

When he yanked on the doorknob, the door flung open without any resistance, because another person was pushing it open at the same time from the inside.

"Oh, sorry, man!" said the other guy, emerging from the opaqueness of the steam. "Wait a minute, Gear Guy?"

"Tracker? Man, am I glad you're still alive!"

"What are you talking about? Of course, I'm alive, you saved my life, remember?"

"Well, yeah, but since you never showed up this morning, I thought you might be dead."

"Dead? Why would you think that?" Tracker confessed he didn't have the slightest idea what Gear Guy was talking about and it appeared they had some serious catching up to do. "But let's go outside and sit on the porch. It's more comfortable, and we can celebrate that I'm not dead."

Gear Guy pointed to Tracker's head. "You don't really wear your hat in the shower, do you?"

"Not during the actual shower, of course, but hey, it's my trademark," he joked. "And believe me, I wouldn't want you to see what I look like without it." As he moved out of the way to let Gear Guy enter the shower room, he pinched his nose. "Phew! Where have you been? You stink."

Gear Guy was still only wearing a towel when he got back to the dorm room after his own shower, and he explained it would be a while before he could leave the room, because he was washing all his clothes... orders from Mr. Hill."

"Mr. Hill? You saw him again? That's funny." He tossed Gear Guy a pair of sweatpants and a T-shirt. "Here, you can wear these for now. Let's go."

The rain was still pounding down, and Tracker led him to the wide porch which wrapped around the house. Nobody else was there and they commandeered a whole seating area.

"So, tell me about dear old Mr. Wino."

"First, he's not a wino. We got him all wrong. I spent a lot of time with him today, and he was the opposite of the man we met yesterday. The new Mr. Hill was very sophisticated. But, I want to find out if Streamin is alive, first."

"What do you mean? I'm not following."

Gear Guy filled him in on what little he knew about the second body, and that since he'd seen Growler at breakfast, and now Tracker, it only left Streamin unaccounted.

"Gosh, that's horrible! But now it's starting to make sense. No wonder you were worried."

"Where were you, by the way? We were expecting you to join us."

"I'm sorry, I overslept, and when I realized I'd missed the meet up at nine, I decided to go back to sleep. I've only been up an hour, so this is all news to me."

"I figured you probably were hungover, or something."

Tracker protested. "Nah, I was drinking soda water all night. I'm a bit of a lightweight in the alcohol department and didn't even finished one beer before switching. I didn't want to spoil the mood, so I pretended to drink along with everyone else. I didn't know anyone noticed."

"Man, I thought I was the only sober one."

Tracker smiled. "Acting runs in the family."

"You sure had me fooled, but I believe you now. In fact, you're the only one I trust around here."

"I wish I could say the same about you."

"What do you mean?"

"Well, didn't you steal my money last night? When I got here I noticed the pocket of my backpack was still unzipped, and my money was gone. Growler had left, and he and Streamin were sound asleep, so it wasn't them. You were the only one there still awake. Who else could it have been?"

"Are you crazy? Of course, I didn't take it."

Tracker laughed. "I mean, I do remember saying you could have it, but I thought you understood I had to go over a cliff or something, first."

"Search my pack, if you don't believe me."

"Okay, okay. But, somebody took it."

Just then, a maroon pickup truck pulled up in front of the hostel. The passenger door opened and out popped an umbrella. It was followed by Alain de Beaumont. He dropped by to give Gear Guy a pamphlet from the local university.

"Sorry. I didn't mean to intrude. Tracker, isn't it? Listen, Gear Guy, I just spoke to the Dean of the Business School, and he said he'd be happy to talk to you about their MBA program. His contact information is on this pamphlet."

"So, you know the Dean, huh? I'm impressed, Mr. Hill. Gear Guy was just telling me the horrible news about somebody getting killed at Jefferson Rock last night, and we were hoping it wasn't Streamin."

"I do have some news about that, but tell me first what happened up there? After the heroics, that is."

Tracker stumbled a little as he tried to reconstruct what transpired. He'd only been asleep for a little while when a loud snort from Streamin woke him. And that's when he heard someone dashing down the steps toward the church. He figured it was Gear Guy leaving, and he would have called out to him, but he didn't want to wake Streamin.

"It wasn't me. Whoever you thought you heard rushing down the steps was someone else. I left almost immediately after you fell asleep, and besides, I didn't run. I was extra quiet, because I didn't want to wake up Growler."

"My goodness, you boys are certainly considerate," chuckled Mr. Hill.

"Yeah, and I don't know why. I don't really like him."

"Well, if it wasn't you, it must have been him I heard. I wonder what he was doing?"

"I can't imagine," said Gear Guy. "Maybe he was running away after stealing your money."

"Anyway, I decided the slab of rock I was sleeping on was just too hard to be comfortable, and since I was already awake I went back down and checked into the hostel."

"You made such a big deal about wanting to wake up at the lookout, I'm a little surprised you ended up here. It was lucky you got a room without a reservation. They said they were booked solid."

Tracker was staring at the rain and didn't respond.

Alain broke the silence. "Tracker, is there something you don't want to tell us?"

After another minute of dead silence, he turned to face them. "Okay. I confess. I haven't been completely honest with you guys." Alain and Gear Guy both sat up straight to hear Tracker's confession. "All those noises up there gave me the creeps, and I got a little scared, so I came down here. When I didn't find an empty bed I slept here on the porch." He looked back up at them and burst out laughing.

"That wasn't very nice," chided Gear Guy. "For a minute there, you had me believing you were the killer. Hey, but I think you might be right about Growler stealing your money. You weren't there this morning when he dropped a big wad of cash."

"And after I bought him dinner and everything," said Tracker.

Alain coughed.

"Oh, sorry Mr. Hill. I meant after I *offered* to buy him dinner. But what if Streamin took it? He could have faked snoring the whole time. What if he waited until Gear Guy left and then stole it? That could have happened."

"I'm afraid not, guys. I picked up some news about Streamin today," said Alain. "Apparently, he went to the police last night around nine o'clock. He must have slipped away when he walked me out."

Gear Guy wanted to know how he found out.

"A small town has as many eyes as a fly."

"Ha-ha, what a cool expression. Is it original?"

"I wish I could say it was, but it's from *Life on Main Street in the 1950s*, a short story by a friend of mine. But I digress. Seriously, I ran into Ranger Cody today, and he told me."

Tracker interrupted. "Now that I think about it, Streamin was gone from the table a long time."

Alain continued, "At the station, Streamin said that the murder victim from the shelter might be this Red Rover person, and he volunteered to identify him. Cody showed him a bunch of Polaroids of hikers from the albums in the Hiker Lounge. They had the names blacked out, and he picked out Red Rover right away."

"But wait! Becky told us the victim was a local guy. Somebody everybody knew. That doesn't sound like Red Rover," said Gear Guy.

"You're absolutely right. As it turned out, by identifying Red Rover, what Streamin did was rule him out as the victim, because Red Rover and the victim didn't resemble each other.

"Does the name Doug Maguire ring a bell with any of you?" asked Alain. "No? Well Doug Maguire was the name of the hiker who didn't show up at the hostel last night, and you're staying in the bunk that was supposed to be his. I learned his name when I peeked at the registration sheet, while we were standing at the counter at check-in earlier. According to the authorities, it's also the name of the unfortunate young man found dead this morning."

Gear Guy was relieved. "I wonder if any of us knew him."

"I'm afraid we all did," said Alain. "It's just that we knew him by his trail name...Streamin. And he couldn't have stolen your money, Tracker, because they didn't find any money on him."

"But Streamin told us he was going to the police this morning. I wonder why he changed his mind and went last night?" asked Tracker.

Just then she and Hardware sloshed onto the porch. They had been to a little shop next door, but from even that short walk in the downpour they were soaking wet. The colors of her hand-painted hair were running down the sides of her head and mixed with her tears. She looked a fright, and they asked her what was wrong.

"I just don't know what to do. What with some lunatic killing people and bears running around, hiking is out of the question. I rented out my condo for two months, so now I don't have anywhere to live. And just when everything was turning around for me."

A few weeks earlier, Moonbeam had met a guy, and after a passionate night or two together, somehow it was decided they would hike the trail together. Camping under the stars sounded so romantic. They even went shopping, and she invested in equipment and train tickets for them both. At dinner in Harpers Ferry the night before they were to begin their hike, the boyfriend excused himself to go to the men's room and never came back.

The shock had hardly sunk in, and Moonbeam didn't know what she was going to do, when Hardware appeared like an angel out of the blue. Not only did provide the comfort she needed, he seemed eager to hike the trail, too.

"And now, he just informed me that he's suddenly been called back to Europe. He's leaving as soon as he can get a flight."

"Business," said Hardware, nodding and frowning.

"I hate to be a wet blanket," said Alain. "But since you and Moonbeam discovered the body, I would imagine it might be quite some time before the authorities will allow you to leave the country, or even Harpers Ferry, for that matter."

"Now I wish we'd gone to work at the farm," she lamented. "Everything would have been so much better."

"It's not too late," said Alain. "The farm you all are talking about is technically within the town's jurisdiction. You'll be safe there. I'll take you myself. In fact, we can all go in my truck."

"But what about the rain?" asked Moonbeam. "I don't want to have to camp in the rain."

"I wouldn't be too concerned about that," said Alain. "I suspect they will put you all up in their bunkhouse. I understand it's quite nice."

"Let's go, then. The sooner, the better. It's dangerous around here!" said Tracker, jumping to his feet. "We'll run and get our stuff."

"Not so fast!" came an authoritative voice from the side of the porch. It was Ranger Cody.

"Oh, excuse me Mr. Hill. I'm sorry to bother you, but I have a warrant here for the arrest of a hiker known as Tracker. I'm afraid he's a suspect in our murder investigation."

Alain looked as stunned as the others, but he stood up and put his hand on the Ranger's shoulder. "Cody, there must be some mistake. I know these young men, and I'm very certain he..."

"I'm Tracker," he said boldly coming forward. His confident façade took a hit when his voice cracked. "And I've got nothing to hide."

As he read him his rights, Cody produced a set of handcuffs and slapped them on Tracker.

"Ranger Cody, are these really necessary?"

"Tracker, you're being charged with two counts of murder and for grand larceny in the amount of five thousand dollars. Gear Guy followed him out to the squad car. "Is this true? Tracker, tell us he's making a mistake!"

"I'm innocent, I tell you. I can explain every..." he yelled, as the door to the car slammed shut.

30

The wind and rain lashed with a fury until late in the afternoon, when it gradually reduced to a slight drizzle. Around six o'clock Alvaro went to rouse Growler. He noticed his tent was flattened, but Growler was not inside, so he walked to the outhouse and banged on the door. At some time in the middle of the night, Growler had shimmied backwards out of his tent and wobbled across to the latrine. By then he was completely soaked, and he figured the tiny shack would be his best chance at drying out. He was too tall to stand up inside, and there was not enough room to sit on the filthy floor, even if he had wanted to try. As a result, he spent the next eighteen hours sitting on the outhouse seat. Eventually, he fell back against one of the side walls but the stench kept him awake. At least he was out of the pouring rain.

Alvaro kicked at the door again, and announced dinner would be served in a few minutes up at the farmhouse. Growler didn't understand his Spanish, of course, but he unlocked the door and waddled out. Between lying in a pool of water inside his tent and being trapped in the outhouse, he was in a vile mood and smelled horrible.

"Where have you been?" he shouted at Alvaro, waving his hands. "They said meals were included. Me hungry!" The

Chilean just shook his head and gestured for him to hop on his golf cart. On the way back to the house, they made a detour to stop at the barn, where they found Lana Lang lounging on a pile of hay, eating a banana and texting.

Growler jumped off the cart and stormed over. He was so thoroughly soaked his shoes made squishing sounds with every step, and she was more amused than intimidated. He was furious and wanted to know how she managed to get such special treatment. "And where did you get that banana?" he added.

She calmly stood up and brushed off the loose hay sticking to her dry clothes. "Special treatment? What are you talking about? For the record, the banana is mine. I thought to bring my own food." She made a big show of biting off the last piece and chewing it slowly in front of him.

Just then, Tornado and the other two hikers entered through the bunkhouse door. All three were drinking beer. "Man, the water in my shower was so hot, I didn't want to leave," he apologized. "Hope I didn't keep you waiting too long."

"Wait a minute! You, stayed here, too? How come nobody told me about all this?" He glared at Lana Lang.

"You dummy. Alvaro told the same thing to both us, when he showed us where to pitch our tents. He said some awful weather was expected, and we could stay in here if we wanted. Our choice. Anyway, when the rain started, I moved to the bunkhouse. On my way, I noticed you were still in your tent, so I assumed you preferred to stay there. God, you smell like crap."

Growler was pissed at her for conveniently leaving out that part of the translation. Since he reeked, nobody wanted to sit next to him so Alvaro made room for him on a dropdown seat at the back. Then he drove them in a roundabout way up to a large yellow and white striped tent set on the lush grassy lawn off to the side of the old farmhouse. As they neared the tent they could hear conversations inside, and when Alvaro opened the side flap for them, they were astonished to find Gear Guy, Moonbeam and Hardware standing together in a cluster, enjoying hors d'oeuvres and sipping wine.

"How did you all get here?" asked Growler, surveying the tent. "And who do I have to see to get a glass of wine?"

As Moonbeam explained how Mr. Hill dropped them off in his truck, Alvaro produced a silver tray with glasses of wine for him and the others.

Lana Lang was perplexed by the incongruity of using stemware and silver trays to serve hikers at a picnic. "Whose farm is this, anyway?" she asked, but no one seemed to know. A tinkle of a spoon clicking the side of a goblet provided the answer.

"Ladies and Gentlemen," said Alvaro with a thick accent, pulling back a flap at the end of the tent. "Your host, Señor Hill."

"Welcome, welcome, everyone," greeted Alain de Beaumont, with a flourish.

There were gasps, as every guest did a double-take. This Mr. Hill was hardly recognizable as the Mr. Hill they'd seen the night before. Gone was the cheap wig. His silver hair was long and thick and pulled back into a ponytail. A black Barbour wool cardigan sweater, open at the collar, framed the perfect Windsor knot of a fashionably skinny gray necktie, which was stunning against a pristine starched white shirt. He wore tailored gray wool slacks, and in defiance of the soggy ground, highly polished Italian loafers. "Welcome to my farm," he said with a twinkle.

He signaled to Alvaro, who moved the group to the large dining table set in the middle of the tent. A place card at each seat bore a trail name, and the hikers circled the table to find their places. Gear Guy was surprised when he read the card at the head of the table.

"Dr. Hill?" he asked.

"Yes, Gear Guy. Did I forget to mention that I did a stint in graduate school, myself?"

Before taking his place at the head of the table, Alain personally went around to refill their glasses. "I think a nice Côte du Rhône is perfect at a picnic," he said. He winked at Lana Lang. "I like mine served at about eighteen degrees Centigrade, don't you?"

He asked everyone to please remain standing and raise their glasses in a silent toast to their absent friend, Streamin.

"What's this for?" griped Lana Lang. "Why do we have to toast him?"

"Oh, of course, you couldn't possibly know." He took a few minutes to report the sad news of finding Streamin, a.k.a. Douglas Maguire, dead that morning.

"Was it a bear attack?" asked Tornado. "It was only a matter of time, before we saw another one."

"No. It was worse," said Alain. "He was murdered, and I can't imagine why."

"I just remembered something," said Gear Guy. "And it's sending chills down my spine. Last night Tracker tried to talk us into staying up there for the night. And this is the eerie part. I remember Streamin say he had no intention of waking up at Jefferson Rock. I wonder if he knew something."

"Well, he got his wish, didn't he?" said Lana Lang. Then she looked a little remorseful for the remark. "Do they know who killed him?"

"Yes, I'm afraid so. They arrested Tracker for both murders this afternoon. It shocked us all," said Alain. "He seemed like such a nice young man and so well-mannered. And to think he was a murderer all along."

Moonbeam had a theory. "Call it a woman's intuition, but I believe he must be one of those, umm, people you hear about who lead two separate lives. Umm, first, there's the person you think you know, and then you find out there's, umm, a whole side you knew nothing about. What do you think, Lana Lang? You're a woman like me."

Lana Lang rolled her eyes. "Well first, let's get one thing straight. I'm not a woman like you. Tracker wasn't my type, either. A bit too goody-goody for my taste."

"How can you say goody-goody? I mean, umm, he murdered someone."

"Sorry, but I just don't believe it," said Gear Guy.

"Don't believe what?" Growler had been only paying half attention to the conversation. He was starving and preoccupied combining single burgers into doubles. He slathered his super-sized portions with mustard and ketchup. "These are very good. What's your secret, Dr. Hill?"

"No big secret. They're veggie burgers."

"Oh." Growler repeated his question to Gear Guy.

"I said I don't believe that Tracker killed Streamin. It just doesn't make any sense."

"Yeah, but if the cops ran him in, they must have had a good reason. And if he killed Streamin, he probably killed the other guy, too, wouldn't you think?"

"Well, I didn't like Tracker, but I bet they got the wrong guy," blurted Lana Lang. She pointed at Growler. "I still believe you are the killer. I always did."

"Me? Why me?" he snapped.

"Because everything about you is suspicious, the lies, slipping out the back door of the restaurant yesterday."

"The expensive backpack and jacket," interjected Gear Guy.

"Your hands," said Moonbeam, joining in the pile on.

"Look, they didn't arrest me, did they? It was Tracker they wanted, so they must have had a good reason."

Gear Guy had a thought. "Hey, Growler. You slept up there in the church ruins. Tracker said he heard you running down the steps in the middle of the night. Was Streamin still asleep when you left?"

"It wasn't me he heard. Anyway, I wouldn't know. I decided not to stay there after all. It was too spooky. I went somewhere else to crash."

"What are you talking about, Growler? It's lies like this that make everyone suspicious of you. We know you were there," said Moonbeam, giving a side-eye to Hardware. She pinched her nose and made a disgusting face. "We found your, um, evidence all over the place." She pulled his scarf out of her bag. "We found this in there, too."

Alain intervened. "Growler is quite right. The police didn't see a reason to arrest him, and I'm certainly not going to let you put him on trial here at my picnic. But now, considering these unsettling circumstances, I hope you will feel free to stay for as long as you like. And that goes for your boyfriend, too,

Lana Lang. When he gets to town, he's welcome to join you out here. I'm just glad to have everyone, safe and sound."

"Well, I don't feel safe, or sound," she snorted. "And my boyfriend won't be joining me here, either, thank you very much. Because I'm leaving." She slid her chair back from the table.

The prospect of getting on the trail and out of the area suddenly sounded appealing to the others.

"The guys and I have just been talking. We want to get out with you, too," said Tornado. "Our stuff is packed, and we're ready to go whenever you are."

"If you're leaving, I'm leaving too," said Growler. "Um, are we still going to get paid?"

"Certainly," laughed Alain. He gestured to Alvaro, who handed envelopes to both him and Lana Lang. "Please run them back to Harpers Ferry now, will you?"

"I'd be happy to."

"Wait! That guy understood English the whole time?" complained Growler.

"I speak five languages," said Alvaro, placing another plate of burgers on the table.

Growler immediately reached for them. "Dr. Hill, do you mind if I take a couple of these with me for the road tonight?"

"Take what you like. Just make sure you all have your IDs handy. I heard the authorities have mounted a large manhunt, and they're checking everyone, and I mean everyone. Both coming and going."

"What for?" asked Lana Lang. "They've arrested the killer, so the case should be closed."

"Oh, no. The manhunt I was speaking about is to look for William de Beaumont, who apparently is still missing."

"What do you mean missing?" she asked. "I thought you said he was dead. Didn't they just pin both murders on Tracker?"

"No, he's not dead!" said Gear Guy. "It was someone else. Becky, the waitress at The Beanery, told me it was some local guy and not de Beaumont."

Lana Lang shrugged her shoulders and shook her head. "How come a dumb waitress knows more than the cops?" she grumbled. "So, that means he's still around here somewhere then, doesn't it?"

"That's what I've been saying," said Gear Guy.

"Well, I'm certainly not going to screw around with a bunch of bureaucrats and checkpoints," she said looking peeved. "I'll just take my chances and leave on foot."

"Yes, that's a good idea. You won't have to endure all that red tape of producing an ID," said Alain.

Hardware didn't want to put up with all those delays, either, and he announced he would take his chances on foot, too. He reminded everyone he had a plane to catch. Then he gave Moonbeam a little peck on the cheek. "You don't mind if I go with Lana Lang, do you?"

Moonbeam grabbed his hand. "If you're leaving, I'm going with you, at least as far as the airport." Then she glared at Lana Lang. "I don't know. Maybe I'll fly to Berlin with you, too, baby."

"Who said I was going to Berlin?"

The flashing lights of a police car pulling up next to the tent, and the car door slammed, interrupting the conversation. Growler panicked and leaped to his feet, spilling his glass of wine and knocking over his chair. As he dashed out of the tent he whispered, "I've got to use the bathroom!"

The side flap opened, and Tracker entered the tent with a grin was so wide his silver capped tooth sparkled. "They had to release me," he said. "I showed them the receipt for the money I got wired. I'm a free man!" Then he yelled over to the other side of the tent. "It's okay, Growler. You can come back in, it's just me! Hey, is there any food left?"

"That's terrific to hear, Tracker. We've all been worried." He called for another toast.

"What about the murder rap?" asked Growler, as he took his place at the table again. "How did you get out of that?"

"Some junior level person bungled the paperwork. Turns out I wasn't a suspect. It was all a big mistake."

"Wait a minute! Dr. Hill, didn't you tell me that the authorities had rounded up everyone on the trail?"

"That's right. Everyone for fifty miles in either direction."

So, with Tracker in the clear, that means the killer must be around here too, doesn't it?"

"That's right, and so is that billionaire," said Tracker. "They identified the body at the shelter, and it wasn't him."

31

"I was terrified, Suzen. It was so weird to see this guy aiming my own knife at me. He had a strong arm and threw it hard, too. If it hadn't grazed the one tree and ricocheted off another, it could have done some serious damage."

Suzen remembered the call from Will like it was yesterday. It was such a relief to hear his voice, after being worried about him for so long. She also found the excitement in his voice a bit frightening, as he gave her the blow by blow of how he'd been rescued.

By the time the knife hit him, the blade had already rotated a few times, and it was only the handle that hit his head. It hurt, and he wasn't sure the guy heard him yell when he went down.

"He probably thought he'd killed me, so just he didn't bother to check."

After the initial sting of the knife subsided, and he thought it safe to get up, he found his way to the meeting place he'd seen on the map. He picked his way through the woods for about thirty minutes before he heard his uncle calling him. It was the first time he had heard the name François in months, and he knew he was safe.

She'd had a different agenda for that call and intended to bring him up to speed on the foundation's current initiatives. But he didn't seem to be paying much attention. He kept bringing the conversation back to the excitement playing out in Harpers Ferry, and to his uncle, who he referred to as amazing. He also told her he had already developed a couple of theories about the killer, but if his uncle had one of his own, he wasn't letting on.

"I'm fascinated by how he can maneuver people into volunteering information about themselves. Here's what I mean. For the first two days, he wore this goofy wig. The color was lame, and it didn't even fit. On top of that, he put on this drunken act. He told me the act worked for him dozens of times before. Oh, and he's fearless, too. I mean he puts himself all alone right in the middle of all these suspects, knowing one of them is a paid assassin!"

Suzen wondered what exactly it was in the de Beaumont blood that attracted them to such risky behavior. But she stopped short of making him promise to be careful in the coming days. Instead she wanted to talk about Plan B and hear specifically what the medical team learned after they examined him.

"Suzen, it worked! Plan B worked!"

The coating of the large capsule was meant to dissolve within a couple hours after he ingested it. Had it behaved properly, the tiny transmitter inside would have begun sending its signal earlier than it did, and it would have helped search and rescue teams locate him before he was assaulted.

In theory, they wanted their experimental transmitter to send its signal about a hundred yards. Through a forest on a steep mountain trail in the dark, a hundred yards would add a significant advantage for search and rescue. In actual experiments, the maximum distance other scientists had transmitted a signal using a nano-device like theirs was only thirty feet. But they had gotten much closer to their goal, and they hoped for the best. It was only their Plan B.

Since the transmitter was inside his body, it needed to be self-powered, and the capsule he swallowed came with a nanogenerator. Those were not experimental. In both tests and in actual practice, vibration-driven nanogenerators already scavenged mechanical vibrations from all over the body and turned them into electricity. And they didn't require much. Scientists had built nanogenerators that self-powered from something as subtle as the vibrations of a person's own blood flow. However, the nanogenerator in Will's stomach would need more than subtle vibrations to work.

What was new in Plan B was a larger capacitor, one that would store enough energy to transmit its signals much farther than previous models. Will was so fascinated by the implications this technology had for surveillance and medicine, he became an active investor in one of the leading companies in the field. His hike created the perfect excuse to be a test subject.

"So, a few things didn't quite perform as we planned. The capsule took much longer to dissolve in my stomach, and I know we can easily tweak the gelatin to fix that. Because it took longer, it delayed the release of the transmitter and the other nano-devices until well after I set up camp. Sitting quietly at the campfire didn't create the required level of vibration for the nanogenerator to produce enough energy. The scientists assumed I would be much more active, and I would have been if it hadn't been for the creep who hovered over me.

"I overate, too. I had just restocked, and because I didn't want to waste anything I decided to cook it all. Even after sharing some of it with the psycho, I ended up eating way too much, and all that partially digested food apparently surrounded the device in my stomach. They said so much food wouldn't have impeded the transmission of data, but it created a different, and unforeseen problem. The type of food and quantity I ate cushioned the nanogenerator from the vibrations it needed to power it on.

"Fortunately, these are all problems we can fix for the next time."

The next time. Suzen didn't like the sound of that.

32

Alain didn't have to ask the stunned guests. The implication that both de Beaumont and the killer were at large was an occasion for more wine, and he made sure their glasses were refilled.

The Chilean approached the table and whispered something in Alain's ear, causing him to excuse himself. He returned moments later with Ranger Cody, who was conspicuously wearing earbuds connected to a small metal device he held in his hands.

"I believe you all know Ranger Cody, don't you?" asked Alain. He looked around the table for affirmations that never materialized. "Cody is working on the murder investigation, and stopped by to tell us about this little gadget. He held up the device. "Does anybody know what this is?" More blank stares. "Never mind. He's going to give us a demonstration."

"Do I have to stay?" asked Lana Lang. "I want to get out of here soon."

"Actually, ma'am, yes you do," said Cody.

Well I hope it's not going to be a long speech," she groused.

"Then I'd better get right down to business. This little thing works something like a Geiger Counter."

He explained that instead of recognizing metal, it picked up something that emitted a different kind of frequency. Before he turned it on, though, he informed them there was a person among them who knew how it worked. He paused and slowly looked around the table to each person, before continuing.

"Is it one of us?" asked Gear Guy.

"No, no." Cody abruptly spun around and handed the device to Alvaro.

"Are you kidding me?" grumbled Growler. "Why do we have to hear him?"

"Because Dr. Gomez can explain is better than I."

Though his English was flawless, and he spoke slowly, it didn't make a bit of difference to his audience. Fast or slow, the complex programming jargon was Greek to most of them, and their eyes glazed over in no time.

"I still don't understand a word he says," complained Growler. "Even when he's speaking English."

"He probably forgot to tell you that one of the five languages he knows is computer language," said Alain. "I'm sorry if it is over your head."

"He was just referencing JavaScript," said Hardware, pronouncing it like *YavaScript*. "It's basic."

"Well, can someone translate it for us dummies?" snickered Gear Guy.

The device was complex and Alain agreed to dumb it down a bit. He explained the gadget picked up certain frequencies, frequencies emitted by specific objects, in this case, the labels embedded in some of the clothing and gear belonging to the missing hiker.

"It has to be de Beaumont," said Gear Guy. "The article in the newspaper said some of his equipment and clothing had his Doodad labels in them. But why would his stuff need to be found? Wouldn't he still have his own gear with him?"

Ranger Cody acknowledged they were talking about the same individual. And it was unfortunate they had reason to believe some of the billionaire's things had been separated from him. Cody's assignment was to scan the belongings of every hiker in Harpers Ferry.

"I was planning to start in town, before I remembered Doug Maguire told me that he and a bunch of hikers were coming out here to the farm to work."

Lana Lang suddenly seemed more interested. "You mean Streamin actually did go to the police? When?"

"Last night, around nine o'clock, as I recall. The information he gave us was very helpful."

Ranger Cody turned it on. Even from across the room, the beeps coming through the tiny speakers of the earbuds were loud enough for everyone at the table to hear. He brought it closer, and the beeps got louder and faster. When he pointed it at Dr. Hill, it went silent. The same for Tracker. It started again when pointed it at Growler, and when he aimed it at his jacket and backpack, the beeps came so fast they blurred into a steady screech.

"I told you he was a criminal!" yelled Lana Lang. "This proves he stole those things from the dead French dude." She stood up. "And I've got more proof. Look at this!" She produced her cellphone and held up the screenshot of Growler.

"Leon Agronsky, a/k/a Leonard something, a/k/a Lonnie something. He's all over the Internet."

Growler went for her. "That's fake news. I'll kill you for this!"

In a surprising move, Hardware jumped in front of Lana Lang, and shoved Growler to the ground.

"See? What did I tell you?" she squeaked. "Keep me away from him. He's dangerous."

"And to think of all the times we laughed when we called it Growler's stuff." Suddenly, Gear Guy stood up. "Wait a minute! I just thought of something. That means William de Beaumont's trail name is Red Rover. It's got to be."

"I don't know what's happening here. That thing is mistaken. I didn't kill anybody!"

Alain stepped in. "Nobody is accusing you of killing anyone, Growler. But what Ranger Cody would like to know is how you ended up with young Mr. de Beaumont's backpack and jacket. Did he give them to you?"

Growler looked around the table to gauge his audience. "Yes. Yes, he did."

Just then, Ranger Cody produced a small, cheap backpack and set it on the table in front of Growler. "Would you like to change your story?"

As Growler sputtered the beginnings of a denial, Cody produced the store receipt for it and all the other things Growler bought that day in the big box store.

"Apparently, you made quite an impression on the store clerk. Oh, and it seems you paid for all this with a credit card that was also reported stolen. The same card you used to rent the car that injured that boy."

"Ranger Cody is making some serious allegations. It might help if you told everyone how you ended up with Red Rover's gear?" asked Alain.

Growler shifted uncomfortably in his seat. "Okay, look. So, when I got to this campsite the other night, there was a guy sitting on a log facing the fire. There were only a few coals burning, but there was enough light that I could see he was slumped over, like he was sleeping. I didn't want to scare him, you know, by like suddenly standing next to him, so I called from across the clearing."

Growler's stomach started to rumble, but the guy didn't seem to hear that, either. It was getting cold, so he quietly added another log to the fire.

There was a pot of noodles or something on the ground in front of him. Whatever it was, it looked good, and he was starving. So, he asked the guy if he could have some of it. By then it was obvious the guy was sound asleep and couldn't hear a thing, so he went ahead and helped himself. He remembered the one-way conversation he had was kind of funny.

"I even told him he was a darned good cook."

"So, you complimented the guy and then killed him for his food and his backpack?" asked Lana Lang.

"No! I keep telling you, I didn't kill anyone."

He still thought the man was sleeping, and he figured if he played his cards right he just might finish eating it all and scram before he woke up. But when he reached over to grab the guy's canteen, he accidentally brushed up against him, and the guy teetered right over onto the ground. But he still didn't wake up.

"That's when I finally put two and two together and figured out he was dead."

"Now we know he can add," mumbled Lana Lang.

"It was late, and since there was nobody else around, I thought I might as well eat the rest of it. Like I said, I hadn't eaten for a day or two."

"Yeah, the last time was probably when you bummed dinner off me," interjected Tornado. "I remember your sad story about bears eating all your food, or somebody stealing your pots and pans, or something. Just so you know, I didn't believe you then."

"You didn't?" asked Growler, gulping down the rest of his wine. "It was terrible. I was lucky those bears didn't go after me."

Alain refilled his glass and snickered. "Yes, yes. I'm sure it was terrifying. But we still want to know how you got the backpack."

"I was still cold, it was probably because of the cheap piece of crap jacket they sold me."

The coat Growler bought hadn't kept him warm or dry. He noticed the guy on the ground was about his size, and the guy's jacket looked warmer than his own. While he was at it, he slipped off the guy's long-sleeved T-shirt, too. It was insulated. Then he said he spotted the green backpack. There was a lot of good stuff in it, but the reason he took it was because it was better than the one he had.

"So, you ripped off both his backpack and his coat. What a creep!" said Gear Guy.

"Look. I was just trying to survive. Besides, he wasn't going to need any of it anymore. Anyway, I left him all his cooking stuff and his tent!"

Growler was about to leave him lying there, when he felt sorry for the guy. He threw the body over his shoulder fireman-style and took him up to the sleeping platform.

"Yech," said Moonbeam, putting her fingers in her ears. "This is too weird for one day."

"You don't know weird! Imagine having a dead man's head flop and bang into your back every time you took a step. I let him keep his hat, and I pulled it down to cover his face, trying to be respectful. Then I covered him with his tarp."

"So, I guess that's when you left this little backpack of yours they found next to him," said Ranger Cody.

"I remember you told me you traded somebody something for your stuff. Some trade," said Tracker.

"Why would anyone believe a word he just said?" Lana Lang turned to Ranger Cody. "Officer, the man you are looking for is sitting right there. Now, are you going to arrest him, or not?"

Ranger Cody said he wasn't under any orders to arrest him. If there was sufficient proof, some other authority would take care of it. His only job was to locate the stolen items, and now that he'd found two of them, he asked Growler to hand them over.

"How am I supposed to hike the trail without a backpack or any of my stuff?" he asked, and Ranger Cody referred him to the Swap Box at the Hiker Lounge.

"Your stuff?" sighed Gear Guy.

Cody said there was still another item they were looking for, and he reactivated the scanner. This time, he pointed it directly at Hardware and then at Moonbeam, and it remained silent. It made no sound either when he aimed at Tornado and the other two hikers, either.

"How about seeing what it does with him?" asked Growler, pointing at Gear Guy. "He's the one who's so interested in hiking gear."

Ranger Cody slowly turned the scanner back past Hardware and Moonbeam and aimed it directly at Gear Guy. It didn't make a peep, and Gear Guy asked why everyone was so surprised. He certainly hadn't stolen anyone's gear. "It would be a sacrilege."

The scanner started squawking again when he pointed it at the last remaining person in the room, Lana Lang.

"What? Me? What the hell is going on?" she barked. "That dumb thing must be on the fritz."

Growler laughed at her predicament and suggested maybe she was the thief. And the killer. Ranger Cody, meanwhile, announced the scanner was picking up the label in her sweater.

"It's definitely wool, but I confess, I don't know the brand," said Gear Guy. "But it does look like a man's sweater."

Lana Lang was incensed. "Nice guess, genius. I told you in the restaurant that I like to wear my boyfriend's clothes."

Moonbeam came to her defense. "I wear men's sweatshirts all the time. They make my chest stand out. These, um, tits of mine have always driven men crazy. Sometimes, umm, they can be a real curse. Know what I mean, Lana Lang?"

Lana Lang reached down and pulled her sweater off, revealing a long-sleeved insulated t-shirt covering average to smallish breasts.

"No, um, I don't. Here, take it!" She tossed the sweater to Ranger Cody, who caught it in the air and left. "Like I said, my boyfriend gave it to me."

She'd had just about enough of all the accusations and wasn't sticking around the farm any longer. She got to her feet. It was so dark that even if there were rangers out there she didn't see a problem sneaking past them.

"I'm getting tired of all the insinuations and insults to my character. I'm leaving now, too," said Growler. Then he stuffed his pockets with burgers and anything else he could scavenge from the table.

Tracker wanted to leave, too. After all the drama in Harpers Ferry, he wanted a change of scenery.

Since that was what everyone wanted, Alain was happy to accommodate them. He knew a spot where they could easily enter the trail under the radar at that hour, and he and Alvaro would be happy to take them all there.

He suggested they get their things together and meet in an hour. "And wear dark clothing, if you have any. You'll be less noticeable.

33

How did everything get so screwed up? If I didn't kill de Beaumont, then who the hell was it? Not that it matters now. Since he's still alive and around here, I should probably stay and finish the job. But, now that Tracker has been released, the cops don't have a killer. And who knows what that guy Streamin told them. I'll try again another time. Better leave now, while I still can.

34

"The killer is in our midst," said Alain. "I can just feel it."

Suzen was confused. "What makes you so sure? A little while ago you weren't convinced you had all the possible suspects. I've been going over the list you gave me, and it makes me wonder if we missed another hiker or two in the drone sweep."

"You mean like Lana Lang's fictional boyfriend?" joked Alain.

"Really? You don't think he exits?"

"I have a theory, I'll give you in a bit"

In the meantime, she wanted to review the suspects again, since they'd narrowed them down a bit. Gear Guy was at the bottom of the list. His fingerprints came back clean, and he seemed squeaky clean. There was still his obsession with Will, and Alain suggested it might be a ploy to get closer.

"Yes, but let's not forget he saved his life," she added.

"That could have been staged."

Since the prints for Tornado's guys were clean, too, and Tornado reported that there was nothing about either of the two hikers that were the least bit suspicious.

Growler's fingerprints pointed to a modest rap sheet, which kept him in a position on the top of the list, and Alain was certain the cash Growler dropped at the café was money he stole from Streamin. Initially, Alain thought Growler wasn't smart enough to be the slippery and calculating assassin that eluded everyone for so long, but now he was starting to have his doubts.

"He's quite good at manipulation, Suzen."

"If he's so masterful, why did he allow himself to get caught for all the petty crimes? I don't know anything about your business, Alain, but if Growler had just committed a hit and run, and we know he did, I don't see why he would further complicate things by committing a murder."

"That's a good point and still a big mystery. Up to now I've wanted him to look guilty, to let the real culprit make a mistake. When the time comes, we'll bring him in on the other charges, even if he's not the killer. Want to hear my current thinking?"

Alain' new theory was that the local boy was looking to score some cash and maybe some new gear, and he got wind of a hiker with expensive taste. He thought François had some money in his backpack, and that's why he wanted it. I doubt he intended to kill anybody, but he ended up getting killed himself.

So, the assassin must have known to look for someone with François' basic description and carrying his gear. He would have built the scanner Alain found to help locate François by his labels. He killed the local boy thinking it was François, because the boy was wearing François' coat. The killer took the sweater and the watch, because we know they got tracked leaving first, and he ran away, which would be consistent with leaving the scene of his crime.

Lana Lang insisted her boyfriend gave her the sweater she was wearing, and that ended up belonging to François. Since

Streamin saw her with Hardware on the trail, it might follow that Hardware killed the guy, stole the sweater and gave it to her.

"So, you think Hardware is the killer?"

"It looks that way to me. And furthermore, I don't believe either Lana Lang or Moonbeam has any idea how dangerous he is, so, we've got to keep a protective eye on them."

Suzen was still confused about the strategy of dropping off everyone in town. "Aren't you running the risk of letting the assassin get away? Whichever one it is?"

"I've got it covered. Anyway, we're not just letting them out anywhere. We're going to drop them off at the ruins of the arsenal. It's right in the middle of town and only a few feet away from a footpath that takes them a quarter mile along a railroad track across the Potomac River into Maryland. They'll be captive the entire way. If, for some reason, the assassin doesn't reveal himself by the time the group reaches the other end, I've arranged to have them all picked up and brought in, and we'll start all over."

"Before I forget it, I wanted you to know the guys will have everything back online in a couple of hours," said Suzen. "They're sorry it took so long, but the virus was quite elaborate. I'll let you know as soon as it's up."

"That's good, but I'm not sure it will be helpful at this point. As you know, most of François' stuff was found. How some of it got to each person is a mystery we won't be able to solve until this whole thing is over."

"See if this photo helps. It's a clip from the security camera footage, and I just received it now, while we've been talking."

Alain's phone vibrated. He smiled and shared the screen and the video clip with his team.

"Ladies and gentlemen, meet our killer!"

35

It was a short trip to the base of Washington Street, and the Hispanic pretended to take a back way to avoid detection. It was nearly midnight, and Harpers Ferry was sound asleep when the truck pulled to the curb beside the ruins of the old Arsenal, made famous by John Brown. The wind blew in strong gusts as everyone spilled out onto the cobblestone street. As they collected their gear, Alvaro gave them directions. They were told to follow the path under the viaduct and head straight over to the large iron bridge, and the walkway would take them across the bridge to the C & O Canal on the Maryland side of the river. Shortly afterward, they'd find the entrance to the Appalachian Trail, and it would be easy to disappear.

The iron footbridge shared the span with active railroad tracks. In addition to regular train traffic, during the day the footbridge was popular with tourists and locals who walked it to enjoy the spectacular view of the two rivers merging below.

Growler didn't waste any time. He took off at the first opportunity and sprinted around the others and onto the bridge.

"There he goes," said Gear Guy. "Running away again. He just can't stop looking suspicious."

"Loser!" snapped Lana Lang.

Two red lights marked the railroad tunnel on the other side of the bridge, and Growler used them as a guide and never looked back. At the other side, the train tracks and the footpath separated. The railroad headed straight ahead and into the tunnel, and the pedestrian section bent away from it to the right, where it stopped at the top of a broad circular iron stairway. Even in the dark, Growler could read the sign and the arrow pointing down for the C & O Canal.

He took one last look behind him, glad he'd outrun everyone. It felt good to be finally back in control again. As he started down the spiral staircase, he thanked his lucky stars he had been able to extricate himself from yet another mess he managed to create. He didn't know where the canal or the Appalachian Trail would take him this time, and he didn't care. He was going to take their advice and disappear. Quickly. Maybe this time he'd settle in Philly. He knew some guys there who might be able to set him up.

The iron stairway clanked under his shoes as he raced down the steps. The wind had picked up, and he was glad there was a railing. It was very dark, and as he landed on the last step he had to squint to make out the arrow on the small sign in front of him. He made the turn and followed the path a short distance where it passed by more crumbled brick ruins. The long sprint across the entire quarter mile of the bridge had left him breathless. His lungs were hurting, and his heart was pounding. He was alone and decided he could afford to rest for a few minutes. He closed his eyes.

"Raise those big hands of yours, sir, and don't try any funny stuff!"

Growler didn't recognize the voice behind the stern warning, but when he felt her pistol jab into his back, he knew the woman meant business. Without moving his torso, he slowly turned his head around to see who it was. Agent Lucille "Lucky" Myers looked a lot different in her police uniform than she did undercover in her waitstaff apron at the White Horse, but Growler recognized her. With a fluid motion that came only with years of practice, she slapped on the handcuffs and read him his rights.

"From the look of things, you've been a very busy man!" she said, as another officer took him into custody and led him away.

Moonbeam and Hardware were still at the truck, and they were arguing. He wanted to go on alone, and she was begging him to take her with him. Each time he tried to walk away, she tugged on his arm to make him stay. She was crying. He remained insistent and cold.

"You've changed," she wailed.

"You're a whiny little bitch," he countered.

Lana Lang, watching their tiff from her position against the hood of the truck, decided to add a little fuel to their fire. "If you're coming with me Hardware, you'd better come now, because I'm leaving."

Moonbeam's heartache turned to rage, and she swung around to face her. "This is all your fault!" she screamed. "You've been trying to steal him from me the second you set eyes on him!"

"Oh, brother!" sighed Lana Lang. "I'm out of here." She had run out of what little patience she had at the start, and remembering Dr. Hill's directions, picked up her gear and headed straight for the bridge, leaving the couple to finish their spat.

"Ow, you're hurting me!" howled Moonbeam, as Hardware yanked his arm from her grip.

"I'm going with her!" he yelled. He turned to leave, but a voice made him stop.

"Not so fast, young man! We've got a few questions we'd like you to answer." The demand came from the other side of the truck.

He ignored the request and barreled past Moonbeam, until he was tripped by Sergeant Rebecca 'Becky' Wilson, who stood over him with gun drawn.

She produced a warrant. "Search him," she ordered. "Now!" A van materialized at the curb, and two agents shoved him inside.

After the heavy rain the water level was high, and a bright moon made it easy see the raging river. Strong winds added to the turbulence below, and gusting crosswinds made it difficult to walk on the footbridge. Tracker, Lana Lang and Gear Guy were about a third of the way across the bridge when they stopped to wait for the winds to die down.

The power and majesty of the rivers below was too spectacular not to appreciate, and the three of them leaned against the railing to soak in the view.

Back in the van, agents searched Hardware's pockets. "Well, looky here, boss," one of them said, handing Alain the thumb drive he found. Alain calmly instructed them to send it to their lab for immediate analysis. The agent laughed and suggested that maybe Hardware should have picked the name Software, instead.

"Or Hacker," said Alain. "And to think he was on our payroll for a while. I can't wait to tell the others in his lab how he ended up." Then he remembered Hardware's watch. It was the perfect opportunity to take a closer look. When Hardware wouldn't hand it over, Alain instructed an agent to remove it from his wrist.

"Hey, what are you doing? Be careful! I paid good money for that thing." he said, resisting her efforts.

It only took him an instant to verify that Hardware was telling the truth. His Epix was a different model, and he handed it back with his apologies. "Book him on two counts of homicide."

"Are you crazy?" yelped Hardware, banging on the sides of the van. "I didn't kill anybody."

On the bridge the wind picked up again, and a strong gust of wind whipped horizontally and caught the bill of Tracker's baseball cap. As it loosened from his head he grabbed for it, but he was too late. It and its fake black pony tail flew up into the air, and the three of them watched it sail out over the river. In the confusion Gear Guy found himself face to face suddenly with a very different looking person. The man who stood before him now sported a thick full head of auburn hair.

Gear Guy was astonished. "Tracker?" he stammered. "You're I can't believe I didn't recognize you. You're Red Rover!"

Will decided he really had nothing to lose by telling the truth to Gear Guy at this point. They would be going their separate ways soon, and the killer had been arrested.

"Yes, I am. There's a perfectly good reason why I've been in disguise, and I'll tell you one of these day."

"So, Growler's backpack and jacket were yours all along, weren't they? I knew the odds of two people with that limited-edition pack were low."

Lana Lang became interested. "Does that mean you are also the French guy everyone was talking about?"

"No," he said, correcting her. "Well, yes, but actually, I'm Swiss."

His clarification was interrupted by a loud scream, coming from the entrance to the bridge. Moonbeam was yelling for help. Without thinking, Gear Guy and Will turned to run to help her, but Lana Lang grabbed Will's arm and asked him to stay.

"Oh, she's just being dramatic again. Don't you think Gear Guy can handle her by himself? You have just become the most fascinating person on the planet, and I want to know more about you."

Gear Guy didn't mind, and he took off back across to the West Virginia side of the bridge. When he got there, Moonbeam told him Hardware had been arrested by mistake, and she was hysterical. She needed Gear Guy's help to get him released. He told her Dr. Hill would know what to do, and asked if she knew where he was. The mention of Hill's name caused her to burst into tears.

"No, don't get him involved! I think he's the one that's behind all this!"

Alain was frustrated. He was still in the van with Alvaro. "Now, I'm starting to have doubts. I was so sure Hardware the killer, but his watch took me by surprise. We know he planted the virus, and I guess I always assumed the same person would be the killer."

"Well, one of them around here is the assassin," said Alvaro. "They all can't be innocent."

Alain's phone rang, and he wasn't sure why he answered it. He'd been ignoring his phone all day. It was Suzen with the news that Will's tracking system would be back up any second.

"Not that it really matters, now, since he is with you now, and you have the killer. I'm sorry it took so long. But someone from Bangkok has been trying to reach you all day. Said it was vitally important. Check your phone for his message."

Alain's face fell when he saw all the messages he'd gotten during the past couple of hours, including the multiple identical ones from his contact in Bangkok, all labeled URGENT. He clicked on the first one.

Forget Le Mauvvais. It's La Mauvaise you want!

Alain's mind raced. La Mauvaise. Of course. Thailand. Plastic surgery. Sex reassignment. Eighteen months in hiding was just about the right amount of time for a transition. Now he was alarmed. He'd convinced his nephew that Hardware was the killer, and the whole time it was Lana Lang!

"Where's François?" he shouted.

Alvaro pointed to the bridge. "He told me he was going to cross with everyone and would come right back."

"Make sure everybody is back in their places," Alain yelled, as he raced off to the bridge.

Will and Lana Lang were still engaged in conversation, and she was her doing her best to show off her softer side. As they stared at the churning water below, she began her seduction. It started with her hand on the small of his back. Slowly she inched her way up to his shoulders, where her hand rested before she dared to rub his neck lightly with her fingers.

"They tell me I give a great massage," she cooed into his ear, as she moved directly behind him. "You seem so tense. Is this helping?"

Will didn't know what to make of her sudden attention, and he didn't care. What he did know was that he was mesmerized by two opposing forces. The violence of the water below, and the tenderness of her touch on his neck.

Her attention made him a little self-conscious, and he dealt with it the way he always did, with a joke. "You know, Lana Lang, under that crusty exterior you're really not such a bad gal."

She was directly behind him now, and both of her skillful hands were massaging his neck. Revenge was close enough to taste.

Men are so easy.

At that precise instant, two hundred and sixty-five miles away on the twenty-seventh floor of the GeoFibre Foundation office in New York City, lights on the wall map twinkled back on, as its computer booted back to life and instantly established a connection with a new controlling server operating from a secret location in Switzerland. In less than a split second, the server triggered a command.

The deafening screeching noise from the watch Lana Lang was wearing startled them both, and her hands, poised for her signature move, instead knocked into his head. She lost her concentration, and as she tried to recover her position, Will spun around in time to catch her in the act.

Gone was the tenderness he felt earlier. What he saw standing before him now was a vicious killer. She reached for his throat, and he pushed her away. She came at him again, and he fended her off before managing to knock her down. Before she could scramble to her feet, Alain arrived and stood defiantly between her and Will.

"Well, well, well. La Mauvaise, I presume?"

"Who are you?" she bristled, surprised at someone making the connection.

"I'm the one you really want to kill."

"You! I should have known. You and your damn picture," she growled. "You made me do all this."

"I've got to hand it to you. You had excellent work done. Too bad you didn't pay your Bangkok doctor what you owed him. He might not have squealed."

Her eyes darted left and right to assess her exit options.

"Hey, we've got your boyfriend back there. I'm not sure what to call him. He goes by so many names."

"He's all yours. He was sloppy and got caught."

"Speaking of sloppy. I'd say you lost your touch. You killed the wrong man up at the shelter, and then we found the tracker you left at the fire."

"His fault, too. He said that piece of crap would make my job easier. I'm working alone from now on."

"You're not going to work at all. I've got you this time." He pointed behind her. "You're trapped!"

She looked over her shoulder and saw Lucky charging toward her. Then she flipped around and saw that de Beaumont now had Alvaro and Tornado standing next to him as reinforcements to block her way.

"You're delusional," she smirked, and took off running straight at Lucky. "I'll be back for you."

"You'll never make it!"

Lana Lang sprinted about twenty yards and stunned them all when she made a quick cut to the right and vaulted the railing like it was a pommel horse. She flung herself out into the pitch-black sky, down into the uncertain waters below.

Alain and the others rushed to the railing, but they were too late, and it was too dark to see the powerful Potomac River sweep up her body and discard it into the confusing currents of the confluence.

Epilogue

Two days later

Thanks to the proliferation of whitewater rafting centers situated along both rivers, there was no shortage of kayaks when Alain's team was deployed to the river to search for Lana Lang.

Considering the river's high water level and surge, she hadn't been carried as far downstream as they calculated. But judging from the extensive punishment her body took and the known currents, river experts believe that Lana Lang was first pummeled in the Whitehorse Rapids past Bass Rock, before her wild ride took her past the Bird Sanctuary Islands via Miller's Hole. They estimated she would have sailed on through toward the Weverton Gates Ruins had she not been slowed down by a submerged tree. Failing to grab onto a branch, Lana Lang probably floated several yards further, where she would have ricocheted off a huge rock. In the end, she managed to get tangled up in a large vine which encircled her neck.

At her autopsy, it was determined she experienced a slow death, as she struggled to free herself in the strong current, as the vine strangled her just off a small island known as Paradise.

The autopsy also showed that Le Mauvais had not undergone a complete transition. From the waist down, Lana Lang was still all man.

"I have to hand it to her. She did only what she needed to change her appearance and get back in her game as soon as possible," said Alain, as he hung up from his call with the medical examiner.

Will said he still felt foolish for falling for her seduction act on the bridge, but by the time they were crossing the bridge, everyone was certain that Hardware was Le Mauvais.

"When they arrested him back at the truck, and I figured that was that. Even a little later, when my hat blew off and my cover was blown, I didn't think anything of it. It never occurred to me that Lana Lang would be a threat."

"I bought into her act, too," said Alain. "The fact that I never considered her a suspect was completely my fault. I assumed we were looking for a man. Talk about thinking inside the box. That assumption clouded my thoughts so much, I didn't even pull her fingerprints. She had a convincing American accent, but she did make some grammatical mistakes, and like most Europeans, she didn't like cold beer."

Once they got her prints, though, Suzen was able to do a lot of digging as on Lana Lang as well. She found out that in addition to being a skilled assassin, she was first an accomplished hacker. Hardware met her in one of those murky corners on the dark web, back when she was a he and known to the world as Le Mauvais. When they discovered they shared the same dark side, Hardware agreed to help plot her revenge against Alain.

While he was transitioning, Hardware was to get himself hired in the GeoFibre lab in Switzerland. It turned out to be easy.

They were always looking for exceptional engineers at their Montreux lab, and Hardware was one of the best. He kept his ears to the ground, and once he caught wind about the hike and got access to the label technology, he and Le Mauvais set the whole elaborate scenario in motion.

"He admitted everything," said Alain. "Collaborating with Lana Lang, inserting the thumb drive to sabotage the tracking system. All of it."

Alain hoped to bring Growler back into custody alive, too, but Mother Nature had other plans. After Lucky handcuffed him at the Maryland side of the bridge and turned him over to a local police officer for safekeeping, she got called back urgently to the bridge. While she was charging toward Lana Lang, somehow Growler managed to overpower the cop and get away back onto the trail. While his escape was an inconvenience, no one was particularly concerned. They chalked it off as a delay. Growler might have been an accomplished conman from Staten Island, but he was so unskilled at hiking and camping they knew it wouldn't take long to find him again.

"It turned out to be even easier than they thought, thanks to Moonbeam who ran into him the next day on the trail."

"Moonbeam? What was she doing up there? Last I heard she was completely distraught about Hardware's arrest."

"Never underestimate the resilience of that woman," added Alain. "She met another guy in a bar that night, and apparently by noon the next day she was back on the trail with him."

A little over an hour into their hike, they stumbled onto Growler's savaged body. Sometime during the night, one or more bears brutally tore him apart.

Gear Guy was astonished. "So, those stories really were true?"

Alain smiled. "What was true was that bears did want his food, just like the poster said. It was just that to get to it, they had to get him first. Apparently, they have a taste for veggie burgers. Before he left my farm, Growler stuffed his pockets with them."

Suzen was still confused. "With all their elaborate planning, I would have thought, Hardware or Lana Lang would have known what you looked like, Alain. If she was so eager to get revenge on you, why wasn't she able to recognize you?"

"It's all about context," said Alain. "Never in a million years would she expect to find me on a farm in wild and wonderful West Virginia."

"Well, I found it hard to believe nobody picked up on the name Tracker," added Suzen. "I thought picking that name was extremely risky."

"Speaking of names, you know, after all this, I still don't know what to call you," said Gear Guy, turning to Will. "You have so many names. Which one do you want me to use? Tracker? Red Rover? Or, maybe one of your real names?"

Will laughed and pulled out his old standby answer. "Take your pick. I answer to all of them."

"Yeah, even to Frank, the truck driver."

"I almost forgot about Frank. Playing him was my favorite role. I wish you could have seen me."

"I wish you could have seen me playing your controlling wife on the other end of the phone call," said Suzen. "I have to admit that was fun, too."

Gear Guy excused himself. He had an appointment with the Dean of the Business School. Thanks to the de Beaumonts, he'd be entering the next term to finish his MBA. When only the three of them remained, Will made a confession.

"You know, reliving the experience just then made something all too clear. Honestly, I don't know if I can go back to work at the GeoFibre Foundation."

"Suzen was understanding. "I can handle things. There's no rush. Take all the time you need."

"No, that's not what I meant. I'm fine. But all this was so exciting. I loved every minute." He paused. "I'm afraid I'd be bored back at the Foundation."

"I don't know," said Alain. "My line of work can be dangerous."

"Yeah, but as it turns out, hiking was a little dangerous, too."

"Touché!" laughed Alain. "Seriously, though, I may have a solution to your dilemma. Coincidentally, this morning a colleague and I were having a high-level discussion about an upcoming assignment. I suggested the Foundation might make the perfect cover for any number of delicate projects. He agreed.

"Anyone want to hear about it?"

CPSIA information can be obtained
at www.ICGtesting.com
Printed in the USA
LVHW01s1650080518
576441LV00001B/222/P

9 780999 255629